# A BEGINNER'S GUIDE TO DEATH, DEMONS, AND OTHER AFTERLIFE DISASTERS

## DEMONIC DISASTERS AND AFTERLIFE ADVENTURES
### BOOK ONE

SHANNON MAE

A Beginner's Guide to Death, Demons, and Other Afterlife Disasters

Copyright 2023 Shannon Mae

Amazon Edition

Formatting by Tammy, Aspen Tree E.A.S.

Cover design by Tammy, Aspen Tree E.A.S.

# ACKNOWLEDGMENTS

Thank you first and foremost to Scott, who kept telling me I ought to write a book of my own already. So I did. Your encouragement gave me the motivation I needed to get started, and your endless inspiration kept the words flowing. I would never have started writing without your belief in me. You have helped me grow as a person, and I am so thankful for your presence in my life.

Thank you to Jennifer Cody; I couldn't have done this without you. Words cannot describe how happy I am that I once wrote a review that you read and reached out to me about. Writing and publishing are daunting prospects, and I cannot thank you enough for alpha reading, offering much needed advice, and answering every single (sometimes ridiculous) question that I had for you. I could not have asked for a better mentor, and I am honored to work with you. You are my writing guru, and I appreciate you more than words can express.

Thank you to the unparalleled Tammy B PA from Aspen Tree E.A.S. You are the other reason this book was able to come to fruition. Thank you for reading and offering endless encouragement, for handling all the details my brain simply could not, and for putting up with my vague ideas on covers and formats and websites. I could not have accomplished everything that goes along with publishing without you. You are simply amazing, and I am so blessed that you are on my team.

Finally, thank you to Nicole for beta reading. You caught my sometimes ridiculous errors (I shook my head at some of the mistakes I missed!), gave invaluable advice, and were wonderful to work with!

Writing may seem like a solitary process, but my team of support made this book possible. I love you all!

# BLURB:

**Adam:**

Adam is not having a good day. First, he finds out his very long time boyfriend has been having an affair. Then, his dramatic exit becomes a little too dramatic when he ends up dead. To top it off, he finds out that the afterlife isn't at all what he expected (he has no desire to learn to play the harp, thank you very much). Fortunately for him, some afterlife bureaucratic screw up ends him up with the most smoking hot demon he's ever seen, and he decides he's keeping him. Maybe the afterlife won't be so bad after all.

**Minos:**

As Judge of the Damned, Minos has seen all sorts of human depravity over his endless existence. When a beautiful, shining soul pops into his chamber for judgment, he knows it's a mistake. The human, however, seems quite content to hang around, and it isn't long before Minos decides he just might decide to keep this one. Minos isn't the optimistic or happy sort, but he can't help but be caught up in the whirlwind that is Adam. When forces beyond his control want to return Adam to his designated afterlife, Minos decides that will not be happening, heaven and hell be damned.

Tags: A very grumpy demon meets his match in a snarky, sunshine-filled human; not all angels are nice; Limbo is the party place to be; the afterlife is run like a corporate office, complete with red tape, pointless memos, and high levels of frustration; Minos has a tail and knows how to use it.

# READER WARNING:

This book is intended for mature audiences only. That means there are some very steamy times between men. There are some light spanking scenes and a mild power exchange during sex, but all sex acts are completely consensual and fully enjoyed by everyone involved. And there's a demon tail, and the demon knows how to use it.

# CHAPTER 1

# ADAM

Adam pulled open another drawer, flailing jeans and sweatpants and khakis onto the growing mound on the bed, shouting along with the music blasting through the bedroom. *I threw your shit into a bag and pushed it down the stairs.* If Tim were here, Adam would've been more likely to push Tim down the damn stairs.

He came across Tim's hideous whitewashed jeans—the ones with the million "artful" rips in them, and he thought quite seriously about making a few new rips. Maybe cutting the whole ass off. After all, it was apparently open for business for anyone.

With that the angry buzz faded, and Adam's eyes teared up. He shut the music off and sat down on the spare inch of hideous purple comforter (Tim's idea, of course) not covered with clothes, picking up the iPad. The iPad that had been cloned to Tim's account yesterday after a stilted, awkward, and mostly silent dinner.

Tim: *I so wish you had been there with me tonight. The sunset over the water was truly beautiful and I wanted to share it with you.*

Morgan: *I'm sure it was. The picture you sent was amazing. The escape*

1

*room with the kids after work was fun. Thank goodness for Josh, or we never would've gotten out.*

Tim: *I'm sure. I've never done one before. We'll have to try one together someday.*

Morgan: *Absolutely. I have every confidence we would find our way out lol. And if not, we'd have plenty of fun being stuck together \*wink emoji\**

Tim: *I hate to say it, but I've got to head to bed. I love you Morgan, and I miss you.*

Morgan: *I love you as well. Miss you so much. Goodnight buddy. You mean the world to me.*

Tim: *Goodnight dearest. I can't wait for the amazing future we're going to have together.*

"*Buddy?* Who the fuck calls the person they're having an illicit affair with *buddy?* What the fuck? Is he a damn elf? A little?" Adam mumbled to himself. So, he had some... interesting tastes in reading. You had to get your kicks somewhere when your sex life was practically nonexistent. And really, Adam thought Tim acting like a little would make perfect sense, because he barely ever did anything for himself.

Maybe Morgan could take care of him. Maybe he would take over paying his car insurance like Tim's mom and dad. Or maybe he would foot the bill for Tim to follow his dreams and go back to college and take a twenty thousand dollar pay cut, like Adam had. "Sure, Tim, follow your dreams—you don't need to pay me half the rent anymore for the townhome," Adam said, staring at the damning messages on the iPad.

Never mind the fact that Adam *knew* Morgan. He was Tim's fucking boss. Never mind that Morgan was *married*. To a WOMAN. With three kids.

And Adam had known something was up. Sure, the late meetings were a clue. And the hour long phone calls with Morgan that showed up on the shared phone bill (which Adam paid for, of course). But Tim insisted they were friends. Colleagues. And didn't Adam *want* Tim to have friends? Wasn't Adam always encouraging Tim to get out more?

And it's true, he was, because Adam was a ray of fucking sunshine, Tim's biggest cheerleader, and Tim was a grumpy motherfucker.

And ok, the sex had been a problem. But Adam just kinda thought maybe that's what happened when you were in your late 30s. And maybe it had been quicker and easier to get off to porn by himself than to have sex with Tim. It was just always the same. All Tim was interested in was blow jobs. Not even a fun shared sixty-nine kinda thing. Your turn, my turn. Tim never even wanted to share fantasies. What guy doesn't want to share their fantasies with their partner? And so after eight years together, Adam figured maybe Tim was just a bit of a prude. But he loved him. They had history together. They never fought. They weren't perfect, but they'd been happy. Sort of. Mostly.

The door slammed on the bottom level, then Tim's footsteps echoed on the stairs.

"Hey babe, you doin' some cleaning?" Tim asked as he walked into the room, loosening his tie.

"You fucking prick," Adam hoarsely grated out.

"What?" Tim stopped in the process of slipping off his shoes. He could never leave them by the damn door like Adam asked. Had to drag mud and shit all through the house. What an odd detail to infuriate Adam right now. But he figured just about anything would infuriate him right now.

"You FUCKING PRICK," Adam shouted, throwing the iPad down at his feet. "How could you? How could you after everything?"

Tim's face paled, but he set his jaw as he picked it up and read what was on it. Finally, after a long pause, he whispered, "Well, you have to admit we haven't been perfect lately."

"Yeah, we haven't been perfect because you've been FUCKING YOUR BOSS. Who is married to a woman, by the way. And has kids. But you have this amazing future planned out, don't you?" Adam got up off the bed, walking over to the closet to ruffle through it for his gym bag. Which, yeah, was buried somewhere because he didn't really ever go to the gym anymore.

"He's leaving his wife. I was going to tell you. I just didn't know how." Tim shrugged, dropping the iPad onto the bed. "I'm so sorry, Adam. I can't help how I feel. We just... fell in love."

"You asshole," Adam whispered. "You just *fell in love*." Adam did the obnoxious thing Tim hated where he put finger quotes around his words. "And just when is he leaving his wife and three kids? Hmmm?"

"The divorce will take a couple years, but it's in the works. And they sleep in separate bedrooms."

"You're a fucking moron, Tim. A divorce doesn't take 'a couple years.' I bet he hasn't even told her. Does she know about you?"

"Of course not," Tim stiffly replied. "We can't say anything until the divorce is final."

"Well isn't that fucking convenient." Adam started pulling his own clothes out. A couple pairs of pants, some underwear and socks, some shirts, throwing the stuff into the bag. "You're such an idiot. He isn't getting divorced. I bet they don't even sleep in separate bedrooms. He isn't leaving his family for you, Tim."

Adam's eyes started to tear up, but he wouldn't give Tim the satisfaction of his tears. "But thank you. Really. Because who knows how many years I would have wasted listening to you complain about *everything*, supporting you through every endeavor, being your ray of fucking sunshine, only to get half your attention and your grumpy ass mood. Who knows how much longer I would have wasted living this half life where you gave me *nothing* and took *everything*. You are a selfish shit, and Morgan can fucking have you." Adam giggled then, half hysterical. "If he even wants you, which is doubtful. I was the best thing in your life and you fucking threw me away. Good luck, asshole."

Adam threw the duffel bag over his shoulder, walking out of the room. "I'm going to stay... somewhere. Pack your shit and get the fuck out of *my* home. Maybe you can sleep at Morgan's. Maybe you can stop by and see just how not getting divorced he actually is."

He took the steps two at a time, and by the time he was walking out the front door, he was gasping from running down the stairs and from the tears running down his face. He threw his stuff in the car, started it, and peeled out of the driveway. Fuck the neighbors.

By the time Adam was getting on the highway, he was sobbing and looking for a radio station that played something angry or depressing or break-up worthy. Then there was the blare of a horn, lights, and Adam didn't remember anything else after that.

# CHAPTER 2
## MINOS

Most days, Minos loved his job. Finding the perfect punishment for the evil humans heading into the underworld was a pleasure, and he was quite creative at his job. Torture could come in so many forms. People thought physical pain was the worst, but not really. Psychological torture—that was where Minos excelled. People's worst fears, their worst experiences, all laid bare. And there was a certain cosmic justice in making the horrible people who came before him undergo what they had done to others. It was balance, and it was beautiful.

But lately, he just seemed to be falling flat in the creativity category. Take the sniveling, sobbing coward in front of him now. He had wet himself when he'd seen Minos, which was usually the case. You'd think all the current horror movies would prepare them for a demon, but perhaps on the screen wasn't the same as the actual experience. And of course they got physical forms so they could wet themselves, or shit themselves, or vomit, or cry. Really, all the bodily functions got a little tiring after a while, but it was part of the hell experience, and Minos prided himself on delivering the perfect postcard experiences for those who deserved them.

Take the judgment room itself— he lounged on what was practically a throne, and yes, perhaps it resembled human bones just a bit. And the dark stone walls and floor, aside from making for easy cleanup, gave a nice look of despair to the place. It was all very bleak and dreary and appropriately fear-inspiring.

"...and then I went to the nursing home and I told all my mother's friends about the retirement fund that could double their money..." the short little man kneeling in front of him continued, still sobbing.

Ugh. He hated white collar crime. Sure, this guy deserved hell. He was a selfish piece of shit who had only ever done anything for himself. He had stolen from his own family, from friends, from people in a nursing home, as he was currently describing. He had never cared about anyone but himself. His only love was money.

He was just so... uncreative. There was so little to work with. He didn't *like* rapists or murderers or the truly evil, but he *did* like finding ways to make them suffer. That was a fun day's work. This was just... dull.

"Send him to the pits for torture. I'll review his case in a week or a year or... whenever," he sighed out to the lesser demon standing beside the man. The pits were *so* blah, but he just didn't have it in him to feel motivated to think of something more creative. He could see the demon's look of disappointment. They enjoyed a little more creativity too. Ah well, maybe the next one would be more inspiring. He sighed. Probably not.

A beautiful woman with dark, curly hair and a lithe figure walked through the doorway to his judgment chamber. She was wearing a long, pale Grecian gown that showed off her curves, and she had a smirk on her face. Minos sighed again as she gracefully folded herself into the chair that was at the far end of the room.

"Pandora, I'm not judging you," Minos sighed out. He rubbed his eyes, the start of a headache forming. "You shouldn't even be in Limbo. You got your pass to head upstairs decades ago. Or has it been centuries at this point?"

"Please, darling, I am *not* heading upstairs. Have you been up there

7

lately?" she asked, pulling a small figurine and a carving knife out of some secret pocket of her dress and beginning to whittle away at it.

"Obviously not, Pandora. I don't think I've been to the multi-department coordination conference rooms since our joint flogging on making sure humans are in the right afterlife for their religious beliefs and deeds. As I recall, the reincarnation department was in quite a bit of trouble over turning someone into a cockroach for a next life."

"Now if it had been an actual flogging, that might have been fun," she winked. Minos only rolled his eyes as she continued. "But that's just my point. It isn't any fun upstairs. There's all these rules, and team building, and productivity, and everyone is always feeling so *accomplished*. Darling, I have no desire whatsoever to accomplish anything. And don't get me started on the music." She stopped whittling and turned to face him, her face lighting up. "Did you know I have an entire radio station named after me topside? Isn't that fitting? I so often deejay the Limbo parties. I bet someone who was dead for a few minutes came up with that name after a brief visit to our orgasmic partyland."

Minos rolled his eyes again. Limbo *had* become quite the party atmosphere in the last few centuries. Of course, there were quieter parts of it for the introverts, space to have lots of self-reflection before deciding where they were going next. What was becoming a problem, however, was that people weren't deciding where to go next. Pandora had somehow become Limbo's defacto leader somewhere in history, and who wanted to move upstairs or to reincarnation or to ghosthood, or to wherever a person believed they went after death, when Limbo was such a good time?

But that wasn't Minos' problem. At some point the powers that be, whether it came from upstairs or downstairs, would decide it was an issue, and then they would get to handle it. All he knew was that it wasn't going to be his problem. Souls in Limbo were not evil enough to require his judgment. Sometimes they felt they deserved punishment, but it wasn't Minos' job to dispense it. Kushiel dealt with those people, and from the look of some of them after a session with Kushiel, he expected both parties felt quite renewed afterwards. Not that Minos was jealous or anything.

"Darling, have you been listening to me?" Pandora asked. Obviously, he hadn't been. He rolled his eyes again. Yes, he was even getting annoyed at himself with the eye rolls now. He felt like that teenage girl who had killed all those people. She had epic eye rolling tendencies, as he expected all teenage girls did.

"No, Pandora, because you shouldn't be here, because I'm *not* judging you." He paused for a moment, finally noticing exactly *what* she was carving. The large, protruding horns, the very long tail wrapped around one leg, just as Minos' tail was wrapped around his leg now, the nicely honed physique (if he didn't say so himself), but... "Pandora," he growled out.

"Yes darling?" she asked, looking up at him innocently. He swore she tilted the figure to face him head on.

"Pandora, is that supposed to be me? Are you making a D&D figurine of me?" Minos growled out.

"Why yes, I am. Isn't that flattering?" she purred at him.

"Pandora." His growl was practically subvocal now. "Why is it *smiling*? I am the Judge of the Damned. I do not *smile*."

"You wouldn't believe how difficult it is to carve such intricate details, you know. And perhaps it's wishful thinking on all our parts. You used to smile in such a creepy way when you gave out just the right punishment. We've all practically forgotten what your lovely little fangs even look like." She whisked the figure back into her gown before continuing. "Minos, you need a break. Legion are even talking about how you're burnt out, how your punishments have been a little... uninspired as of late."

"What in Limbo are you doing chatting with demons?" Minos asked, flipping his legs off the side of his throne and facing Pandora. If she'd been down below without authorization... "AND I do not have 'little' fangs," he added.

"Calm down, Minos. Limbo has the *best* parties. Even some of the upper demons come up for a good time nowadays." She leaned forward, whispering, "We *might* even get some angels from upstairs." She sat back again, raising her voice once more. "And that's what I'm trying to tell you. You need to get out. Try something new. Take a break. Darling, you love your role, but it's become work for you. And everyone needs a break from work. You just need some inspiration. Maybe a little fun. A lovely young man or woman to take some carnal pleasures with. A chance to show off your not-so-little fangs. Some time to eat, drink, and be merry." She raised her hand before Minos could interrupt her. "Yes, I know you don't need to eat or drink or sleep or fuck, but for the sake of the underworld, Minos, you need to take a break."

With that, she rose and sashayed her way out the door she had entered from. Minos waited for the next evildoer to be escorted in, but none of his demons brought anyone. If that wasn't telling, he didn't know what was. Obviously his lack of inspiration hadn't gone unnoticed. Perhaps it was time to take a little hiatus from judgment.

# CHAPTER 3

# ADAM

He was sitting at a desk. There was a lovely young woman holding some type of tablet sitting across from him. And everything was white. The desk, the walls, the floor, the chairs they were sitting on, her dress—all white. He looked down at himself and saw white pants and a white shirt. The material was very comfortable though—linen, maybe? There was a window, and when he looked out he saw a bright blue sky with white fluffy clouds and pristine white walkways interrupted by patches of perfectly green grass. And, he blinked and looked again—was there a group of people playing harps? It sure looked like it.

"My name is Angela," the woman said, and she pronounced it like Angel with an "ugh" sound afterwards. She had blonde hair that looked like she'd just come out of the salon, and he'd kill for her skin. He didn't think he could see a single pore.

"Umm, ok," Adam replied. Maybe he was dreaming. He didn't remember much after storming out on Tim.

"You aren't dreaming," she said. Did he say that out loud? She was still looking down at her tablet. "Now, we have you listed as being loosely affiliated with Christianity, and according to your files, heaven would be your afterlife recommendation."

"Umm, what?" Adam felt decidedly stupid at the moment. He wasn't really sure what the heck was going on.

Angela looked up at him, her brow *almost* creasing with what appeared to be frustration or confusion. "I'm sorry, have you not been through basic afterlife readiness yet?"

"Umm..." Adam started again. He had *no clue* what the hell she was talking about.

Angela sighed, put down the tablet, and folded her hands in front of her. "I apologize, Adam, but you should have been briefed on your death already. According to my files, you were in a car crash. A drunk driver was going the wrong way on the highway, hit your car, and you veered into the side wall and died instantly."

Adam started giggling, probably a bit hysterically, but he couldn't help it. "I crashed my car into a wall? Are you serious?" he asked, managing to stop giggling for a minute. He looked at Angela, but she only stared back blankly. "I was blasting Icona Pop, and I *was* ready to throw Tim's shit into a bag and push it down the stairs, but I didn't expect the song to prove to be so... prophetic. I mean, I am a 90s bitch, but..." he couldn't even finish, as the giggles took over again.

He looked at Angela and realized she was completely unamused with his story. She did *not* look like a fun time. He managed to get himself under control with a few throat clearings, and when he seemed to have the appropriate serious face back on she continued talking. Damn ice queen.

"Now, I am aware this may come as a bit of a shock, but here in afterlife placement, we want you to know that this is only a new beginning, not an ending. Heaven will be quite lovely for you. As you can see, there are even harp lessons," she pointed out the window as she said the last bit.

Adam followed her finger to see that, yes, those were indeed a bunch of people playing harps. "There must be some mistake," Adam said, looking back at her.

"I assure you that there isn't," she replied, picking up the tablet again. "You are quite dead."

"No, I mean, not about that. About the heaven thing," Adam replied.

"Hmm?" Angela asked.

"You see," Adam said, leaning a little closer, "I'm bisexual."

He waited, but Angela looked entirely unimpressed. "Yes, we are aware of your sexual orientation."

"And I have enjoyed having sex with quite a few men. And women. And I've done lots of other sinful things, too." He wasn't about to list them for this prude, though. She did not invite conversation.

"Mm-hmm," Angela replied, looking down again at her tablet. "So you are questioning whether your placement is correct?"

"Yes," Adam said, leaning back in relief. He looked out the window again at the sterile landscape. And the harps. Everyone looked... perfect. They looked like they were playing in perfect synchronicity, and they looked like they had perfect bodies. It was honestly a little creepy. And *boring*. Adam hated boring.

"I see," Angela said, and now Adam thought she definitely sounded miffed, even if he couldn't tell from her perfect face. "And have you killed anyone?"

"What?! No!" Adam replied, but she obviously wasn't done, as she held a hand up in a rather snooty way.

"Forced people to have sex with you? Drugged people against their knowledge? Tortured or abused people? Tortured or abused children or animals? Have you knowingly destroyed someone's life? Have you stolen from those less fortunate than you? Purposely set out to harm someone in a permanent and life altering way? Poured milk in the cereal bowl before the cereal?"

"Angela," a voice boomed warningly from the wall after the last item on the woman's list.

"Well, it isn't natural," she sniffed, looking up as she spoke. She looked back at Adam before she spoke again. "We have a full list of every act and thought in your entire life, and I can assure you that you are most definitely in the right place. Now, I'm sure you'll want to get to being productive right away. Your file shows you are quite motivated, optimistic, and energetic. We have a garden committee, there are the harp players, of course..."

Adam cut her off before she could go any further. "No, I don't think I *am* in the right place. I'm not staying here. I'm not joining a garden club and I'm sure as hell not learning to play a harp. What are my other choices 'for placement?'" he asked, doing the air quote thing even though Tim wasn't here to be annoyed by it. This woman was quickly moving up in his list of people to be annoyed by, though, so he figured it was ok.

"Your *other choices*?" she asked. And oh boy, there was definitely now a wrinkle in her forehead. "You want *other choices*? Fine. Go before the Judge of the Damned, and then we'll see how you feel about *other choices*."

Adam heard the voice booming something from the wall, but before he could even process what it said, Angela had hit something on her tablet, and Adam was fading out of the room.

He was getting really tired of these abrupt transitions. So far, death sucked.

# CHAPTER 4
# MINOS

Minos was sulking. He knew it, too. Pandora had left the door to the judgment chamber open, and it sounded like Limbo had quite the party going on. They did have all the best musicians, after all.

No lesser demons were bringing in any new souls to judge, so here he was, sitting on his throne of bones, legs draped over the side, sulking over the white-collar crime afterlifer who he'd sent to the pits. He was disappointed in himself. It was a terrible punishment—and not terrible in the good, underworld sort of way. He was letting himself down. He was letting all the demons who worked as torturers down. His lack of inspiration was probably rippling down and causing them to be uninspired as well. And no one wanted lesser demons with too much time on their hands. You didn't inspire them enough and next thing you know you had the creation of telemarketers and click bait articles. No one needed more misery like that in the world.

Right in the middle of his pity party (he could admit that's exactly what he was having), a human plopped into existence in front of him. Like three feet in front of him, which was definitely judging territory. Only this human, who was about six feet tall with short, light brown hair, hazel eyes, and a dad bod, as the topsiders termed it, was *not* evil. He could get a sense of those things by now. Plus, no lesser demon accompanying him.

The little guy (ok, so they were all little guys when you were just over seven feet tall) did not stay kneeling, however. He hopped up, looked around at the room, and then looked at Minos. And Minos waited. Any second now would come the screaming. Or the crying. Or the release of bodily functions.

"Oh, thank god," he said, turning from Minos and looking around the room again. He seemed to jerk about and stared at Minos again, looking more than slightly horrified. Minos sighed. A little delayed, but here it was. The screaming would probably be next.

"Oh my goodness, I am *so sorry*," the man said, looking truly appalled but still not screaming. "I mean, I probably shouldn't say the g-word, right? Is that, like, offensive or something? Because you know I would hate to be offensive to anyone, and I really do *not* have any intention whatsoever of going *back there*." He said the last two words with such utter disdain that Minos couldn't imagine what he was talking about.

He knew he should interrupt the guy. Or tell him to step back, at least. Minos had the effect of removing a human's brain-to-mouth filter, which was obviously necessary when you were digging deep into the human psyche. Sure, he could go the more productive route and have it all laid out in writing like they did upstairs, but that just seemed terribly uninspired. And not very scary, either. It was much more fun to make people say every terrible thing they'd ever done or thought, including admitting the things out loud that they barely admitted to themselves.

"Ohhh, you are *tall*," the man said. "Hmmm. And horns. And the facial hair. I'm *such* a sucker for facial hair. I mean, sure, you're like, sort of burgundy-colored, or whatever—gotta admit I expected bright red, but you rock that color. And the *tail*!" The man looked positively delighted now, and Minos still had no idea what in the underworld to say.

"Oh, I read this *fantastic* alien book, and the things that alien did with that tail to the main character!" He started fanning himself. "I have to admit that was a favorite! I must have read it and gotten off to it about a dozen times. And they couldn't have actual sex, because, you know, the alien's penis was like the size of a leg, and just... ouch. Do you even have a penis? Or a vagina? Or genitalia? Or both? Oh! Wouldn't that be awesome—you could have both and be with a man or a woman! I'd love to have both, but I'm guessing I can't just turn into a demon, even if I never go back to that other place again."

The man started pacing around the room, and Minos figured as he got further away, he'd realize what he'd just spilled and be mildly appalled.

"I do love the look of this place though. There you are, all sexy and threatening on your throne of... bones? Are those bones? Oh, that's just perfect. And the dark stone walls and floor. And the flickering candles dripping wax? Just so perfect." He stopped walking, nearly all the way across the room now.

*Ah, and here it finally comes,* thought Minos. Although if he admitted it to himself, he would have to say this was probably the most surprising visitor he'd had in eons. He was a little sad to see the man go, but he was far enough that Minos' thrall wouldn't work, and the door to Limbo was just in front of him, and any second now he'd be rushing out, utterly bewildered by his behavior while in this room.

Any minute now...

"Um..." The man's head tilted, first one way then the other, and then he turned around, facing Minos. "Is that Kurt Cobain? And Jim Morrison? Because it totally sounds like the two of them. Singing together? And I was gonna say that can't be right, right? But it totally could be right, I guess, because they're, you know..." The man walked closer again, and Minos *almost* put his hand up to stop the guy. His finger kinda twitched, so that counted as trying to warn the human, right?

Only he didn't stop at the usual six feet away. He came right up to the throne, actually stepped *onto* the dais, and whispered, "...dead." And then he stared at Minos expectantly.

Before Minos could even formulate a reply—he had somehow lost track of what the question even was—white-collar-crime's lesser demon walked in through the mostly hidden door in the back corner of the room, already complaining before realizing they weren't alone.

"Minos, the *pits*? There are only so many ways to flay skin off a human body, only so many bones to break, and you know how I hate the mess, and they don't ever really feel the burning pain of the guilt they should. That guy stole from old people in a nursing home. He stole from his own mother. He bought himself boats and fancy cars and hired cleaners and cooks and then harassed them while the people he defrauded couldn't afford care or medication. He had no love or respect for anything in the world, and the best we got is the pits?

"And I worked the pits for *millennia* before I got promoted up to Judge of the Damned level torturer, and you're gonna stick me right back..." the lesser demon finally realized they weren't alone and sort of trailed off as he noticed the human, who had turned around and was now partly standing in front of Minos. The demon took a step forward, and the man took a step back, and Minos wasn't sure quite how it happened, but the next thing he knew he had a man sitting in his lap and a lesser demon gaping at them both with utter shock on his face.

"Oh, you're comfy," the man said. "You look all hard and muscly, but you've got a nice lap to sit on. I'm a total cuddle slut, I gotta admit —it annoyed Tim, the prick, because he needed 'his space' when he was tired," the man said, doing this cute air quote thing with his fingers when he mocked Tim, whoever the hell that idiot was.

"But your lap feels nice and secure, and let's face it, I could lose a few pounds—I mean I'm not like horrific or anything naked, I carry it well, but I'm no muscle go—" the man cut himself off abruptly, actually *patted Minos' thigh*, and then continued on. "Sorry Mr. Sexy Demon, no g-word from me! But anyway, super comfy. Ten out of ten stars. Would totally come again." At which point he started giggling.

"Would totally *come* again," he said, stressing the word come and still giggling.

Minos looked at the man, looked at his lesser demon, who looked as confused as him, and looked back at the man. He got another thigh pat for focusing on the human once again, but then the man turned his attention to the lesser demon.

"Hey! I'm Adam. And you are just the shade of red I expected." He turned back to Minos, doing the thigh pat for a third time, and Minos had to admit he was thinking about just putting his hand over the man's—Adam, that was his name, and wasn't that ironic?—so that his hand would just stay on Minos' thigh. "But of course," Adam went on, "burgundy is lovely as well. You wear it so well, and I wouldn't want you any other color." Then he smiled. At Minos.

"Ahhh, sir?" the lesser demon asked, looking back and forth between the two of them. But Minos still had no idea what to say.

"So, is that what you guys do? She did say I was gonna go before the Judge of the Damned, so it makes sense you, like, judge bad people, and I guess you come up with punishments? And physical torture is probably so 1400s, right? You guys probably go all *Clockwork Orange* and tape people's eyelids open and make them watch some horrible show, like *Dance Moms*. Although ok, I did watch a few episodes, but it was like a train wreck, you know? You just couldn't help getting sucked in.

"But obviously that won't work for some guy who stole from his *mom*. And old people. Ewww. There should be a special place in hell for people who steal from old people. Old people are so sweet. And they're just lonely. You know, you should totally make this guy have to take care of ALL the old people. But the crotchety, cranky ones. And the ones who tell the same story five hundred times, and he's gotta listen to it every time and pretend to be interested. And the ones who bitch about stupid shit like Agnes not weeding her garden and her useless grand-children who never visit. And make him clean up all the nursing home bodily fluids, and of course have the bed pans *always* spill on him. And get him the old people with no boundaries, so he's always walking in on naked old people or being hit on by some grandma or flashed by some grandpa.

"I mean, don't get me wrong, I *like* old people in general. But there are some nasty ones. And he should have to, like, spend eternity making up for it by hearing all the boring stories and cleaning their open wounds and just generally helping the people he defrauded. A life of service. Maybe even make him work some retail for old people. Because that combines like the worst job *ever* and the people he fucked over!"

The lesser demon was actually smiling and nodding along with Adam. Minos was just staring at him. Because it *was* sort of perfect. That little white-collar-crime shit would *hate* cleaning bed pans, and it would be a special kind of torture for him to have to actually listen to other people complain endlessly about petty things, all while he wouldn't be able to be mean or yell at them or walk away.

The lesser demon was staring at Minos hopefully now. Adam was staring at him too, and Minos realized the human's eyes were flecked with little specks of an almost gold color amongst the brown of them. And without looking away, Minos nodded. "Yes. What he said," and he barely noticed as the lesser demon hurried out the side door, practically hopping with excitement at creating Adam's special place in hell for someone who defrauded old people.

# CHAPTER 5
# ADAM

OK, so Adam realized that maybe it was a little odd that he was currently cuddled up to a giant burgundy demon. He also realized that he had absolutely no filter on a good day —Tim always used to yell at him that he jumped topics too quickly and he didn't need to say *everything* he was thinking—but this was a little extreme even for him. But demon guy was just so damn sexy, and Adam felt this instant pull towards him.

"You are so damn sexy," Adam whispered, proving that yup, he really did say everything that was on his mind. Oops. But demon guy didn't seem to mind, so Adam gave himself an in-his-head shrug and just went with it.

Burgundy demon was wearing dark leather-looking breeches (he'd wanted to use that word forever, but really, you never saw someone wearing anything remotely like "breeches" in the real world) and nothing else. And he was all muscle and hot sexiness. Adam thought he could lose count if he even tried to start counting ab muscles here. And he didn't usually go for the gym rats, but demon guy was totally the silent, brooding type, and Adam had to admit that was totally his kinda guy. Or demon, apparently.

Tim had been the silent, brooding type. Unfortunately, Tim had also been the type to complain about everything, blame everyone else for his problems, and play the martyr when anything in his life went wrong. Which had been positively infuriating. You couldn't ever get any fights resolved when the other person just defaulted to "Everything is always my fault and I suck." Somehow Tim would fuck up and Adam would end up comforting him.

"You know," Adam said, sort of leaning a little further into demon guy and maybe petting his chest just a bit. He couldn't help it, though. It was a chest that just begged to be petted. He got slightly distracted by that, sort of losing his train of thought, but demon guy just stared at him patiently, waiting for him to finish. "You have a great chest."

Demon guy sort of grunted in response, but he still stared down at Adam and didn't stop Adam from petting his chest, so Adam kept right on doing it.

"I gotta tell you," Adam continued, "that dying was really sucky at first. Well, also, it was sort of funny." He started giggling. "I mean, I was singing along to a song about crashing my car and then BOOM! I crash my car. Well, a drunk driver hit me, so I didn't really crash it on my own, but still—I had the perfect death song!" he finished.

"And then there was that awful Angel-ugh chick. I mean, what a *bitch*. And no, I am *not* taking harp lessons. Or joining your gardening club. And I like women and men, although maybe I go for men a little more, I gotta admit. And I definitely go for gay romance, because that shit is *hot*, and so much fun, and Oh! I have definitely read a few demon-human romances that were totally hot, and Big Guy, you could give any of those characters a run for their money.

"But *anyway*—I was definitely *not* into her, flawless skin and perfect hair or not. She was like this sterile, fake robot. Not an ounce of horniness when looking at her. But you—mmmhmmm," he finished off, sort of wiggling his eyebrows. Because demon guy was definitely giving him all the horny vibes.

"So," he finished up, "I'm totally staying with you." And then he looked up at demon guy and waited for a response. Adam knew it was impulsive to declare such a thing, but hey, he was already dead—what did he have to lose?

Demon guy looked more than a little confused. And Adam still didn't even know his name. "What's your name?" he asked. "And do you have a hell condo or something, or do you just sort of live in here?"

Because this place looked fun, or at the very least interesting, and the last few months *had* been a drag with Tim. Adam realized it wasn't just the sex that had been boring—it had been everything about Tim and their relationship. Aside from the whole dying part of it, ending things with Tim had probably been the best decision he ever could've made. He did like to always make the best of a bad situation. Maybe he'd curl into a ball and cry later, but right now he was snuggled up to a hot demon, and life... or death, rather, was looking up for the first time in ages. He had been stuck in a rut, and now he was damn well going to have some fun.

"Minos," demon guy rumbled in response. Oh, that voice.

"You totally could be a phone sex operator," Adam noted. "And Dante, yeah?"

Minos scowled at that, and even his scowl was sexy. "It wasn't *our* idea to let the writer see things down here, and he certainly twisted things to fit his own beliefs. He was quite the prude, proclaiming most sexual acts unnatural. If anyone who had anal or oral sex ended up in a ring of hell, upstairs would lose most of its population." Minos sort of shrugged after that, and oh, all those rippling muscles. And that voice.

Adam was definitely getting horny, and the white, loose pants he was wearing would probably *not* hide that reaction. Although really, he was in hell, so flashing a hard-on was probably par for the course here.

He wiggled a little on Minos' lap. He was back to the whole genitalia question with that thought. And, since his filter was totally broken at the moment, he asked, "So? What *do* you have? I mean, penis? Vagina? Are you all smooth like a Ken doll down there? Because even if so, that tail still has so many possibilities."

Adam thought Minos might have turned a deeper shade of burgundy. And the guy did not look embarrassed. So Adam gave another little lap wiggle, hoping to see if he got a little poke, and the more he wiggled, the more he was pretty sure that yes, there was something getting hard underneath his ass. Hard and long and thick. Mmmhmmm.

"Adam," Minos sort of growled, and Adam sat still, because there was no denying the warning in that growly voice, but he also got harder himself, because there was definite authority in that voice. Maybe he'd read too many gay romance novels (Tim used to call them his porn books, which wasn't fair, because they weren't *all* sex—some of them didn't even have sex scenes!), but the idea of having a good time with a demon who took charge in the bedroom was *totally* doing it for him.

Adam looked up into Minos' eyes, and at first he'd thought they were black, but they weren't total darkness. They were more like a cloudy, dark night. Pitch black was devoid of anything, but Minos' eyes were alive with possibilities that were just barely visible. It was like there was movement in them and hints of different shades of black. Adam got lost staring into his eyes, and Minos was staring right back, and then his head seemed to dip the tiniest bit toward Adam.

Then those dark lips were pressed to his, and there was warmth, and Adam's eyes were closed and he sighed with pleasure at the simple act of pressing his lips to someone else's. He didn't think he and Tim had done more than a perfunctory peck in months, and this was just so *nice*.

And then Minos parted his lips, and Adam parted his, and they seemed to share their breaths with one another. And the moment after that all thoughts of Tim and *nice* were stripped from his head. Because Minos growled low in his throat, and the next thing he knew their tongues were dueling with one another, their lips slanting this way and then that way for better angles, and he felt Minos' teeth gently bite down on his lower lip, tugging on it, and then he was the one doing the groaning. Then Minos' tongue was spearing into his mouth, and Adam sucked on it, moaning all the while and shivering at the deep rumbles coming from Minos.

He realized he was plastered up against all that hot, hard flesh, straddling Minos' lap and practically dry humping him as their tongues danced with each other, as teeth nibbled and mouths sucked. Adam had always liked kissing, but he didn't ever think he'd been kissed quite like this. He thought he could probably cum just from making out with his big sexy demon.

They parted almost at the same time, both of them breathing heavily, and Adam wasn't really sure why the most magnificent kiss of his life (he wasn't even exaggerating) had ended until he heard Minos speak.

"What?" Mr. Sexy Demon growled out, and Adam thought Minos was talking to him until he realized Minos wasn't looking at him, but rather at a short, yellowish colored demon who must have come in through the side door, because he was standing right next to it. He looked both highly confused and highly aroused. And maybe also slightly terrified when Minos spoke to him.

"Ummm," was all the yellow guy managed to get out before he squeaked a bit and raced back through the door, leaving it wide open.

And that was simply too much temptation for Adam. Because obviously that was the doorway to hell, or the underworld, or whatever it was—and now that Adam had gotten a taste of his big sexy demon (yes, *his*), he was *not* going back "upstairs," as Minos had called it. Minos didn't know it yet, but he had just gotten himself a human.

And with that, Adam jumped off the big guy's lap, bounced off the platform that contained the throne of bones (still so cool), and headed right toward the door that the yellow demon had run through.

He wasn't terribly surprised to feel the heat emanating from the door, and he was fully braced for flames, rivers of blood, and maybe some pits filled with the screams of the anguished and suffering souls. He wasn't particularly thrilled at the thought, but Minos definitely made up for some possible bad scenery, and Adam had gone *way* too long without having anything resembling a good time.

Besides, he figured Mr. Big Sexy would protect him from whatever scariness was through the door. He could already hear Minos getting up and following behind him. Before he could stop Adam from heading into his home territory in some attempt to protect him, Adam raced a little faster through the door.

And stopped dead the minute he made it through.

Because...

"Are we in Florida?" Adam asked.

OK, so it obviously wasn't Florida (although really, wouldn't that explain *so* much??). But the heat and humidity felt the same. And the sky was like a beautiful sunset, although he realized maybe that was just its natural color. He was expecting a blood red sky or eternal darkness or something, and instead he got a pretty sunset sky filled with pinks and maroons and hints of purple and blue.

And he was pretty sure there were palm trees up ahead. And there were definitely condos. He had really been joking about the hell condo, but apparently he wasn't too far off the mark.

"So you guys don't live in caves or anything? No rivers of blood? Pits filled with the screams of the tortured? Waterfalls of fire?"

"This is the section where most demons live. Of course we don't have the pits or rivers of blood here," Minos replied. And Adam had absolutely no idea if he was kidding or not.

"So you totally do have a hell condo? Can we see it? I can't wait to see your decorating taste!" Adam giggled a little at that. At the very least, it would be entertaining.

"I do not live in a 'condo,'" Minos sniffed. Awww, had Adam offended Mr. Sexy Judge of the Damned? He tried not to smile at that. It was just so cute.

He knew it was probably a little weird that he thought everything a demon did was cute. Because Minos was super grumpy, but there was just something about him that made Adam trust him and want to tell him all his deepest secrets and desires. And he figured Minos had probably heard it all and nothing would shock him, and there was something really comforting in knowing that.

After all, didn't everyone want someone they could bare their soul to? Someone who wouldn't judge them? Someone who you could show the worst parts of yourself to, and they'd still look at you exactly the same? And, ironically, he didn't think the Judge of the Damned would think any differently of him no matter what nonsense came out of his mouth. After all, like Ms. Bitchy "upstairs" had stated, he hadn't done anything *truly* terrible. Sure, he had some kinky fantasies and the occasional murderous thoughts, but the first was fun and the second was probably pretty normal (he wouldn't *actually* kill anyone). And if he was a somewhat neurotic, eternal optimist who was slightly obsessive and spilled every thought in his head, he got the impression that Minos wouldn't mind those things.

"Well, lead on to your not-condo, then," Adam said, and he started walking. Because he figured the further he got from the door to hell the more likely it was that Minos wouldn't drag him back out.

"I don't think..." Minos started before trailing off. He was staring ahead where there were a few demons meandering about, some quite normal looking for demons (was that a briefcase in one's hand?), while others looked fully demonic, complete with whips, chains, and possibly even a mace covered in gore. (Ewwww.)

But in the distance amongst the normal sized demons (most of them were *not* as tall as Minos) was one who towered over the rest. He was stone grey, and the guy had actual, literal wings. Like pitch black, feathered, huge wings looming up over his shoulders. His hair was long and dark and he had a whip coiled around one arm. And Minos was staring straight at him. And the other demon was staring straight at... Adam.

Uh-oh.

# CHAPTER 6
# MINOS

*ell shit.*

Kushiel was about the *last* demon that Minos wanted to see right now. Because, first of all, a human was in Sheol, and humans were not supposed to be in this part of the under-world. They weren't supposed to see where demons actually lived—it was supposed to be all lakes of blood and fire. Insert eye roll here. Listening to the screams of the damned got pretty boring after a few centuries, and although the lake of fire was actually kind of pretty, the rivers of blood were just boring. They were sluggishly slow, crossing them by boat always took forever, and the metallic, rotten smell just completed the unappealing picture.

It was hell, after all, so unappealing was kind of expected, and he planned to keep Adam far away from the pits. And the river. But some things were fun. The labyrinth was really his favorite part, and he thought Adam would find it amusing. That's where the most devious punishments were carried out. It was satisfying to walk into an illusion where someone was being punished in a creative and personalized way. Everyone's worst torture was different, and it was justice to see the truly evil people in the world suffering for their sins. If he remembered correctly, he even had someone eternally sitting through a teen pop concert surrounded by mean girls. Adam would love that.

Apparently Adam's ability to go off on tangents was catching, because Minos realized he needed to focus on the *now* problem, not ruminate on hell's more appealing aspects and what Adam would enjoy seeing. He also realized that apparently he had already made a decision—he was keeping Adam.

There was the crux of the issue, because demons did not just "keep" human souls in Sheol, and a large part of that problem was walking toward him right now. Because Kushiel's job was also judgment and punishment, and Adam would most assuredly fall under his purview, not under Minos'. Kushiel got the good souls who felt like they ought to suffer, and Adam was a good soul. Kushiel had perfected this whole bdsm thing over the years with most of his souls, and the thought of Adam being dominated by Kushiel made Minos want to kill him. Slowly.

Which again brought up the fact that Adam should *never* have ended up in front of him. He didn't know who had fucked up upstairs, but he had no doubt that at some point someone would realize the error, and then there would be nothing but problems.

Kushiel strutted closer, actually flaring his wings out a bit—such a show-off—and Minos took Adam's hand in his and pulled the human partly behind him, shielding him with his body. Adam held onto his hand and placed his other hand on Minos' back. He also seemed to sigh in a dreamy way while staring at Kushiel, which only pissed off Minos more. He'd had a taste of the human, and he was not handing him over.

"What do we have here, Judge of the Damned?" Kushiel asked, and yes, he was definitely fluffing his wings out. Using Minos' formal title was definitely a power play, as well. The fucker.

"Why is the Rigid One of *God*, an *Angel* of Punishment, questioning the Judge of the Damned, an Infernal King of the Underworld? This is my domain, Kushiel. You are merely an occasional occupant amongst the damned. Or do you forget your place?"

Adam peeked around Minos at all the throwing around of titles, and Kushiel looked at him with interest. "I do not think this soul is yours, Judge of the Damned."

"He was sent to my judgment chamber, so apparently you are mistaken," Minos replied. *Shit, shit, shit.*

"I think," Kushiel continued, stepping closer, "that he looks like he should be under my... guidance. If he feels the need for punishment, I'm sure I can... *satisfy* those needs."

At that, Adam stepped forward, ignoring Minos' firm grip on his hand. Minos had a moment of panic, because if Adam asked to go with Kushiel, he couldn't very well say no, but he didn't think he could let the human go either. Adam had shaken something loose in Minos and woken him from his state of boredom, and Minos was drawn to him in a way that was inexplicable. Watching him be punished by Kushiel would be torture (and him calling it that was saying something, because he *knew* torture), but he didn't think he could just walk away. Nor did he think he could deny the human what he was justly permitted to have. Good souls got to seek penance with Kushiel.

"Umm, excuse me, but *hell no*," Adam said, surprising both Minos and Kushiel. Minos actually watched as Kushiel's mouth fell open a little in surprise. "I don't know who you think you are, Mr. Rigid One, but no thanks, I don't need a piece of your rigid anything. And I am *not* dealing with any more angels, nope, no thank you. So you can march straight back 'upstairs'"—and Adam did that cute air quote thing with his fingers again—"and you can tell them to *fuck off.* And fluff those wings all you want, Mr. Rigid One, but I am still not going with you for some of your kinky punishment. I got a demon and I don't need another one, thanks."

Adam turned to Minos then, half whispering, "I mean, so the wings are sexy, but don't worry Big Guy, I'm a one demon kinda guy. And he's way too cocky for me. You're all sexy brooding hotness, which is so my jam. He's got the cocky prick energy, and that is *not* my jam. So can we lose him and finish what we started?" Then the little human actually looked back at Kushiel and stared him down. Well, tried to stare him down even though he was shorter than Kushiel.

Minos was once again speechless, and it seemed Kushiel was as well.

Until the angel started laughing. Loudly. A full-out belly laugh that *almost* made Minos want to smile, but he kept his broody look on by sheer force of will (especially now that he knew how much Adam appreciated it).

"By all that is unholy, you've found the perfect match for yourself," Kushiel chuckled. "I wish you luck, brother, in your endeavors with this one. He's feisty. If you need any tips on taming his boisterous nature, let me know."

"I expect I'll do just fine without your assistance, Kushiel," Minos said. He relaxed a bit knowing that Kushiel had turned off the sex appeal and was showing some level of support.

"All the same, what will you do with him? He isn't, strictly speaking, supposed to be here. And I'm still not sure he belongs under your judgment, although he seems quite happy to be there," Kushiel said, looking more closely again at Adam. "In fact, I'm quite sure he doesn't deserve eternal punishment."

Adam huffed. "Well I'm not being eternally punished, so don't worry your pretty little wings about that."

"Humans are not allowed in Sheol," Kushiel replied, looking from Adam to Minos.

"Yeah, but I definitely do not belong 'upstairs' either," Adam said, shrugging. "Minos is the Judge of the Damned. He's creative. He'll figure it out. But I am *not* leaving, so maybe we can just be on our way, hmmm?"

Kushiel looked at Minos, raised an eyebrow, then glanced at Adam and then back at Minos. Minos shrugged and then nodded. Yes, it was a problem. Yes, Adam didn't seem to think so. Yes, Adam seemed to think he was staying. And yes, he *was* staying.

It was amazing what an angel and a demon who knew each other for eternity could communicate with a few expressions.

"Well, then, I wish you luck, brother," Kushiel said. "And I shall send you on your way."

At which point Kushiel opened his wings and surrounded Minos and Adam with them. The feathers became an endless darkness that consumed them, and then, in a blink, the darkness was gone and they were in Minos' home.

*What a show off*, thought Minos with an eye roll.

# CHAPTER 7

# ADAM

Adam wondered if people ever just walked anywhere after death, because all this fading into new surroundings was definitely getting old. And ok, the wing thing had been cooler than any of the other transitions so far, but still.

"Don't you people ever just walk anywhere?" he asked, because apparently the filter was *still* broken.

"And I'm sorry, but I seem to have absolutely zero filter around you. Like usually I'm all about the word vomit, but I *can* keep things to myself. Like I can't help telling you that I totally want to climb on top of you and ride you off into the sunset, and that is something I would usually keep to myself."

And he was about to continue, but then he actually noticed his surroundings. They were in some type of living space, and most of the furniture was grey, but it looked incredibly comfy, and there was a huge window along one wall, and the view was... wow.

"Oh man, is that an *actual* waterfall of fire? Firefall? Lavafall? Because man, that is amazing. And *those trees*. They are just... they are freaking awesome. All reaching branches, and it looks like there's a layer of snow on them, but that isn't possible, right? Because, you know, hell. And fire pouring down some gorgeous cliffs, so snow would totally melt. That is *awesome*."

"It's the ash from the firefall," Minos replied, and when Adam turned toward him, he realized Minos was staring at him, not out the window. And he looked... odd. He didn't have his normal brooding face on, nor was he looking all sexy and ready to jump Adam's bones.

"Ok, what's wrong, because something is wrong. Your normal broody face is missing," Adam said, walking over and wrapping himself around his sexy demon. Yeah, it was totally weird to be randomly snuggling up to someone he had only met that day, but Minos didn't seem to mind, so he was just going with it.

After all, he'd had a rough day. He'd died and everything. Cuddles were totally necessary.

Minos wrapped his arms around Adam, and Adam's head fit just under Minos', so Minos could rest his cheek on top of Adam's head, and it was about the nicest thing Adam had ever felt. He'd never been with anyone tall enough to do this, and it was kinda awesome to be snuggled up to Minos' chest and feel like he was totally surrounded by him.

They cuddled for a few minutes in silence, but silence for too long wasn't Adam's style. "So?" he asked. "What was the look?"

Minos stepped back, and Adam sighed, because cuddles were awesome, but he went ahead and sat down on the couch. And it *was* super comfy. He patted the cushion next to him, and Minos took the hint and sat, and Adam sort of sprawled out with his head at the other end and put his legs on Minos' legs. It was sort of a half cuddle, and this way he could see Minos' face.

"Still waiting," Adam prompted. Because Minos was definitely looking oddly, and he wasn't getting out of talking about it. If Adam had learned anything from his failed relationship with Tim, which weirdly felt like it had happened months ago, it was that you couldn't just ignore shit and hope it went away. Newsflash—it never went away.

"And why does my life seem so far away? Like I feel like I died months ago, not a day ago. It's totally weird," Adam asked.

Minos looked a little more relaxed at that question. "It's how the soul is engineered to process death. Death sends you through acceptance and understanding. It's like you speed through a year of heavy self-reflection, all in a few seconds of time. After that, you would've gone through 'afterlife readiness' if you were upstairs. They love their classes and self-reflection up there." Minos rolled his eyes at that. "Down here we just get on with Limbo or judgment."

"Ahhh, yeah," Adam replied. "That's what she was talking about. Angel-ugh, or Miss Bitchy, was miffed I hadn't been through some course or other and that she had to explain my death to me."

"Hmmm," Minos hummed. "Yes, they don't like deviation from their standards up there. It's rather obnoxious."

"You don't have to tell me, Big Guy. I had to deal with her attitude. And although this is probably the most you've spoken—nice job, by the way!—you still didn't answer my original question about that look on your face. No secrets. I'm not doing the secret thing ever again. Been there, done that, and somewhere there's a corpse to prove it. Because I am totally blaming Tim for my death.

"So spill it. What's up?" Adam asked. And then he just snuggled down into the cushy couch, legs comfortably resting on Minos, and waited. Because he could *occasionally* keep his mouth shut for a few minutes.

"Ahhh, yes," Minos said, and he placed his hands on Adam's legs, which was incredibly nice. Adam had the impression it was partly to touch Adam but also partly to keep Adam where he was. Like he would run away from Mr. Sexy here. Besides, where would he go? The firefall was beautiful, but he didn't think he'd be taking a dip in it any time soon.

"I am the Judge of the Damned," Minos stated. Which, duh, Adam knew already. But he just waited and let his sexy demon get out whatever he needed to say. Because he did *not* look excited about this conversation.

35

"Is this about me being a human and the fact that I'm not supposed to be here?" Adam asked. Because, yeah, apparently he couldn't keep his mouth shut for two minutes. Oops.

"No. Well, that is an issue, but that's something we'll deal with when upstairs comes looking for you. Luce really won't care that you're here. Flouting the rules is kind of his thing, after all."

Adam assumed Luce was short for Lucifer, which was kind of cute, and it was through sheer force of will that he refrained from commenting on the cuteness of it. Because he *really* didn't want to keep derailing Minos until he got to the bottom of whatever was bothering his sexy demon. So he waited until Minos started talking again. And man, it was *hard* not to talk sometimes.

"My 'look,' as you called it, has more to do with your 'lack of filter,' as you phrased it."

"Oh my go—umm..." Because apparently Adam *couldn't* shut up, and he also couldn't stop saying the g-word.

"You can say 'god,' Adam. You won't be struck with lightning or anything," Minos chuckled. And ok, brooding Minos was sexy as fuck, but chuckling Minos was even better, because Adam was the reason that he was chuckling, and that was kind of awesome.

"Oh my god, then! You totally hate my random rambling and word vomit, and I'm *so sorry*! I really thought you didn't mind, and I don't know what's wrong with me, but I can't seem to help myself," Adam prattled, getting more worked up as he went, and by the time he was done he went to move off Minos, but Minos gripped his legs firmly and kept him right where he was.

"Stop," Minos growled. And oh, that growl. How he could go from mortified to horny in two seconds flat was beyond him, but that growl just did it for him.

"I don't mind your rambling. I *love* your rambling. I want to know everything that's in your head. Never feel bad about saying what you're thinking," Minos assured, squeezing Adam's legs. And Adam settled down at that and felt better, because Minos looked passionate about actually wanting to hear what Adam said. Which was kind of cool.

"And that is sort of what I was trying to tell you," Minos continued. "You really *can't* help it. You literally can't. Because I am the Judge of the Damned, and my job is to judge people on their actions, but also on their deepest secrets, their innermost desires and thoughts. In order to know that, people have to be willing to tell me all those things. In fact, people have to feel *compelled* to tell me those things.

"So... I do that. My presence does that. It makes you want to tell me everything. The further you get from me, the easier it will be to resist talking. Usually six feet is fairly safe. Ten feet is a sure bet. But three feet or closer, and you won't be able to help yourself.

"But you need to know that I want to hear all your rambling. I judge the worst, most depraved humans. They tell me all their secrets, and they're horrible. I don't mind, because it's my job, and I find justice for them. There's satisfaction in that.

"But your rambling... it's refreshing. It's like a cool breeze after nothing but stifling air for so long. I love to hear the thoughts in your head. I want to know all your secrets and all your desires, because they are beautiful and sexy and fun, and they show what a good soul you really are. Your thoughts are a candle in the darkness, and I wouldn't extinguish them for all the world. But that doesn't mean I have the right to compel you to tell me things you don't want to." Minos finished talking, and then it looked like it took an act of strength for him to let go of Adam's legs and physically lift his hands from holding Adam there on the couch.

"Silly demon. Do you think I'm gonna get up and move now? If you don't mind the word vomit, if you actually *like* it, then I'm not going anywhere. Because secrets suck, and I've never had a problem baring my soul to anyone—even complete strangers while standing in line at coffee shops. And that's just because I'm bored.

"So to word vomit all over someone who actually *wants* to hear it? Score! Besides, cuddles from you, or even better, some more making out, totally makes up for any demon mojo you got going on that makes me want to tell you everything in my head." And Adam playfully wiggled his eyebrows at Minos at that.

Minos chuckled again—double score for Adam!—and although they didn't start making out (unfortunately), they did look out the window together all snuggled up while Adam asked a bunch of weird questions about hell's landscape and Minos' job and his house and anything else Adam could think of to ask.

And Minos answered all his questions without getting annoyed, and without telling him he had the attention span of a gerbil (yes, that had totally been a line Tim had once used when they were arguing). There were more snuggles and more chuckles, and it was like the best first date that he had never had when he was alive. Being dead had started off kinda sucky, but since meeting Minos, things had definitely been getting brighter.

And Adam thought again that maybe it was super fast and a little weird to feel so close to someone he'd just met, but he was dead, after all, so he was just going with it. He realized that maybe they had it backwards upstairs. Because snuggling on the couch with Minos, having all his silly questions answered, and being looked at like he was the most interesting person in the world?

Well, that pretty much felt like heaven to him.

## CHAPTER 8
# MINOS

Adam and Minos had talked for hours. At some point, Adam had asked about eating and drinking, and Minos had let him know it wasn't necessary but that it was still possible. So Minos had conjured up a bit of a feast (he had been doing a little of his own showing off), and Adam had been totally delighted.

They'd eaten and talked more, and Minos had reveled in Adam's view of everything; he had been fascinated and excited by every aspect of hell. His delight and excitement made Minos appreciate things, like his amazing view, that he'd long grown inured to. Adam even thought Minos' job was interesting, and he asked endless questions. Minos had stayed away from the most gruesome examples of punishment, but he did share some of his more creative labyrinth punishments, and Adam had been completely enthralled by it all.

Somehow Adam had even gotten Minos to agree to let him come to work with him at some point, because, as Adam said, he had done such a fantastic job with white collar crime guy. Adam might even have wheedled his way into seeing the labyrinth, although Minos hadn't promised anything there. He wasn't sure he wanted his Adam anywhere near the experienced torture demons and other higher level demons.

And the human was *his* Adam; Minos was claiming him, and there was no way he was giving him up. He would have to talk to Luce about it, but as he said, Luce wasn't exactly a rule follower. He figured they'd find some way to get around the rules and keep Adam down here. Luce delighted in finding new and creative ways to fuck with the upstairs crew, and when he realized how much it meant to Minos, he would make sure Adam wasn't going anywhere.

Then Adam had asked why he wasn't tired, and Minos had said they didn't *have* to sleep, just like they didn't have to eat or drink, but that many still chose to. Some demons found it refreshing to rest their minds and process their experiences through dreams. So Adam had wanted to try sleeping, and Minos had instructed him on how to put himself into a restful state. When Adam was sound asleep, Minos had carried him into his bed—which he was sure Adam would love. He had laid down and snuggled up to his human, enjoying the body next to him, and perhaps thinking a few lascivious thoughts for when Adam did wake up. He had thoroughly enjoyed their kiss, and he had plans for another quite soon.

Adam was curled around Minos, their legs intertwined, with Minos's arms wrapped around Adam, when he felt Adam start to stir. Minos couldn't help it—his cock was rock hard. The little sighs and groans his human was making as he woke up were going straight to his dick—and yes, he did have a dick. He'd done the vagina thing for a few centuries, and he'd even done both for a while (breasts were such fantastic fun), but the past few decades had him feeling decidedly male, and he did enjoy his cock. And lucky him, his little human seemed to be very into him having one. Because as Adam's body wiggled closer to his, he felt Adam's also very hard dick pressing against his leg.

Adam's hand found its way to Minos' cock, and when he felt the hardness there, he groaned. "Holy shit, you're *big*," he whispered.

"I can adjust the size if you'd wish. I thought this was proportionate to my body," Minos replied, wondering if he had gone with too big. He wasn't unmanageable; at least, the last time he'd played he hadn't had any complaints. Although the last time he'd played... well, it might be a few years, possibly even a decade. He really had been stuck in a rut lately.

"Oh fuck no," Adam answered, and then his hands were working the ties open to Minos' pants, and Adam was tugging them off and sliding his body down, and Minos lifted his hips to help, happy to let his little human explore his body.

Before Minos knew what was happening, his cock was in Adam's mouth. By all that was unholy, he had forgotten how good this felt, or maybe it had never felt this good, because he didn't think he'd ever had anyone jump on his dick with such energy and enthusiasm.

Adam was licking all around the head, and one hand had reached down to cup his balls and fondle them. Adam's other hand was gripping the bottom of his shaft in a tight ring, slowly sliding up and down. After licking like he had found a favorite lollipop, Adam engulfed Minos in his mouth. He dipped his tongue into Minos' slit while his mouth gently suckled on the head of Minos' cock. Unholy fuck, that felt *amazing*, and Minos couldn't help groaning out in pleasure.

When Minos groaned, Adam groaned too, like he was the one who was getting sucked off. Minos watched as Adam literally swallowed down his entire dick, practically gagging himself on it, moaning all the while. It was one of the hottest things he had ever seen. Sometimes he liked to be... a bit controlling with his partners. He enjoyed watching a partner lose themselves completely to the sexual act. It was clear Adam was thoroughly enjoying sucking Minos off; he was fully engrossed in it, attacking Minos' dick with an energy level that matched his personality.

Minos rested his hand on Adam's head, which made Adam moan even louder. Minos saw Adam's hips moving against the bed, bringing himself pleasure as he worked on Minos. He was so beautiful, so unbridled in his passion.

"By all that is unholy, you feel amazing. Yes, little one, just like that. You look so good choking on my cock. Demons, yes, just like that," he growled out as Adam was bobbing up and down on him, his tongue circling the head of Minos' cock on every upsweep. Every time he went down, he sank further onto Minos, taking more into his mouth. Minos felt Adam's throat constrict around the head of his cock, and Minos groaned out in pleasure. That only seemed to spur Adaim on. He stayed with Minos' cock down his throat, moaning and moving his hips against the bed, until Minos wondered if he could even get air —although it wasn't like he could actually die from lack of oxygen, being already dead.

When the constriction of Adam's throat against his dick had brought Minos to the edge, he forcibly lifted Adam's head up. His little human's eyes were blown wide open and watering, and he was gasping for breath. He was beautiful. "You make me feel so good, little one. What do you want? Tell me what you want, and I'll give it to you."

"Oh god," Adam moaned, and he felt Adam tug against his hand. Not to be free of it, Minos thought, but to feel how tightly Minos was holding him.

Minos smiled, replying "Not quite god, but high enough in the hierarchy," which made Adam laugh before he groaned again as he tugged lightly in Minos' grip.

"Tell me, little one. Tell me your desires," Minos growled, and Adam whimpered.

He locked eyes with Minos, licked his lips, and groaned out, "I want you to be the one in charge. I want to get you off and make you feel good. I want you to talk to me and tell me what to do. I want you to suck me while I suck you. Fuck, I want your dick back in my mouth."

It was like this human had been made for him. Minos had no problem being the one in charge. He had so many plans for this man. He would give him everything he desired, and if he desired getting lost in someone else's control, then Minos was happy to oblige.

Minos tugged him up and then flipped him around, which elicited an adorable little squeak in Adam. Although Adam was shorter, their torsos were close enough in size that mouths and dicks lined up beautifully. Before Minos could speak, Adam was back on Minos' dick, sucking and licking. He slid his tongue around the sensitive underside and then up into his slit, and his hand reached down to cup Minos' balls again and caress them.

Minos didn't let the pleasure overwhelm him, because Adam's dick was right in front of his mouth, and he wanted a taste of that perfect treat. It was beautiful—smaller than his, but Adam was shorter than Minos and his dick was in perfect proportion to his body.

Minos swallowed Adam down. What a lovely mouthful it was. He hadn't had the salty, earthy taste of flesh in his mouth for so long, and Adam's cock was delicious.

He wrapped his tongue around the dick in his mouth, curling it all the way around right beneath the head. *The perks of a demon tongue,* Minos thought, as Adam momentarily stopped moving on Minos and simply groaned in pleasure.

Adam's dick jumped in his mouth, and then he moved back onto Minos's dick with renewed vigor. Minos could feel the spit on his shaft and hear the moans as Adam sucked and bobbed on him. His hand circled around Minos as he focused his mouth and tongue on the head of the cock in his mouth, and his other hand was rolling Minos' balls and ever so gently tugging them. The pleasure was exquisite, and having Adam's dick in his own mouth only added to it.

As Minos' tongue tightened beneath the head of Adam's cock, he moved his own head up and down, slicking the shaft with his spit. He felt Adam grow more frenzied and moan even louder.

The pressure was growing inside Minos, and he knew he wouldn't last much longer. Adam's mouth was moving, his tongue sliding, both hands working. The feel of Adam's dick in his mouth, the sounds of his moans, and the knowledge that his partner was feeling so much pleasure sent him careening toward his orgasm.

"That's it, baby. Just like that. Do you want my cum? Do you want me to cum in your mouth? You're doing so good. You feel so good," Minos growled out around Adam's cock. He groaned long and low at

Minos' words and pumped his hips, and Minos tasted the salty yet sweet taste of Adam's cum coat his mouth. His human tasted as delicious as he looked, which didn't surprise him. He sucked and swallowed until there was nothing left.

It was enough to send Minos over the edge of the cliff into orgasm. His body arched and his dick ached in that moment before the pressure was released. With a growl the cum flowed out of his dick and Adam swallowed it all down, still groaning.

Eventually Adam's hips stopped pumping and Adam's own mouth stopped moving on Minos' cock. He felt his little human's dick grow soft, and Adam moved to rest his head on Minos' thigh.

"Holy fuck. Holy fucking fuck. *Unholy fuck*," Adam whispered against Minos' thigh. "That was... fuck. That was just.. Holy shit. I think I'm speechless. I'm never speechless. I always have words for all the things."

Minos chuckled, because even speechless, Adam still couldn't stop talking. Adam looked up at him with something like adoration in his eyes when Minos was chuckling. Minos didn't think he'd ever seen that look aimed at him. Humans looked at him with fear, or loathing, or dejection, or, with the feisty ones, anger and hatred.

He had those who looked at him with friendship, or respect for his work, but what was shining in Adam's eyes right now? It almost looked like love, and Minos had no idea what to do with that.

He pulled his little human up and held him tightly against his chest, their breaths naturally starting to align, and he held on. Adam sighed and burrowed into him, and for once his little human actually *was* speechless. Minos just enjoyed holding him, waiting to see what new and surprising things his little human might say next when the haze of sex had passed.

He thought he might actually be... happy. He wasn't sure what to do with the feeling, so he just let it settle in and decided he'd figure it out later.

# CHAPTER 9

# ADAM

Adam was settled on Minos' lap on the throne of bones in the Chamber of Judgment (it seemed like it ought to be capitalized in Adam's head, and he totally said it to himself like it was). He still couldn't get over the actual bones—it was so totally campy and cool at the same time. And badass. Because Minos was *totally* badass.

And amazing in bed. Holy shit. Because Adam was trying really hard to focus, but he was still sort of blissed out from the sublime experience that had been sixty-nining with Minos. He and Tim hadn't had much going on in the bedroom for years, and he realized that they probably hadn't had *good* sex, like, ever.

Adam had initially liked how laid back about sex Tim had been, but he was realizing that really it had just been boring, not laid back. Adam used to *love* giving blow jobs. Which, ok, he knew some people weren't fans, but he didn't get it. Feeling a hard dick in your mouth, tasting someone's skin and pre-cum, hearing the moans—it was hot. Feeling that dick getting harder as you sucked on it and licked it and used your tongue on it? HOT.

And maybe he had a bit of an oral fixation, because he couldn't

45

seem to shut up, like, ever. But it was also knowing you were giving someone else pleasure. That they were totally into what you were doing. But with Tim, even something he used to love had gotten stale. Because Tim had never seemed *totally* into it. The sex was *fine*, but that's all it ever was. Tim got off, and he got off, but it wasn't very fun or messy or... carnal? One of his favorite activities had become like a chore. And he sort of hated Tim for that.

But Minos had made up for years of boring. Because holy shit, when Minos had started talking to him? Who knew he was such a whore for positive feedback. Because it had *totally* done it for Adam. When he had deep throated Minos and heard him moan, felt his dick pulse—damn. Adam didn't ever think giving a blow job had been so good for him. Even though he had felt his eyes start to water from having Minos' dick so deep, he hadn't wanted to come up, because he had just felt so good and floaty and horny. It was like an out of body experience.

And hey, if ever there was a time for out of body experiences, death was it. Adam snorted at that, and Minos looked at him, but Adam just smiled until Minos focused back on the demon and the human kneeling in front of them.

But Adam went right back to sex brain, and he realized that he was probably into being controlled a little more than he thought, because when Minos had grabbed his hair—that had been hot as fuck. Minos hadn't hurt him, and Adam somehow totally trusted that he would *never* hurt him, but just knowing that Minos was in charge? Total turn on.

He wiggled a little at that. He was definitely getting horny thinking about sex. He had a feeling that *nothing* was off the table with Minos. And he had so many ideas in his head.

Ideas which he was *not* going to blurt out. Because he had barely managed to convince Minos to let him go to work with him. But he had, and so far it had been pretty fun. At first, the demons did a bit of a double take to see him sitting there on Minos' lap, but the humans seemed so focused on Minos that he mostly got ignored. Most of the people were downright awful human beings, and it had felt kinda cool to add in his ideas on how they should be punished. And every once in a while he couldn't help asking the humans questions, but the demons with them and Minos just listened and nodded when he did that, so he thought he must be somewhat helpful, or at the very least not a distraction.

The demons had seemed sort of sullen and... well, tired, he guessed, when they were first popping in. And definitely surprised to see him. But by the third or fourth human, the entire mood of the demons entering the chamber had changed. Word must have gotten around about Adam, because as the judging wore on, the demons seemed gleeful (in a sinister way, of course) when they popped in and saw him sitting there.

Were there water coolers to gossip around in hell? If not, there must at least be break rooms, or maybe some form of a group text or office teams thread, and he figured he was probably the main source of office chatter in them right now. His imagination took him down a whole path of demons gleefully texting one another and gossiping about their boss's love life, and he had to restrain another chuckle.

Everyone had been really nice, though, considering this was hell. There had only been one sort-of incident so far. Before word had probably gotten around about him, a demon had popped in, seen him sprawled on Minos' lap, and the demon had promptly put his hand over the human's mouth who he had arrived with, giving Minos some kind of look. Minos had stared back for a minute and then asked Adam if he'd like to maybe take a quick nap or go back to his place for a bit. He'd gone for the nap, because Minos' lap was comfy, and he really didn't want to go off wandering hell on his own. And who didn't like naps?

He'd woken up as the man was being dragged off, and the demon had looked *really* sinister and scary, and Minos had looked kind of foreboding as well, although he'd had a gentle pat for Adam's arm when Adam looked at him. He figured there were some things he didn't want to hear about, and he trusted Minos to know what those things were.

Adam sighed, and the demon and Minos both looked at him. Oops. It was just that the guy in front of them right now was BORING. He was really handsome, but man, there was nothing going on upstairs. He talked endlessly about all the women he'd slept with, and the money he'd made (not very honestly), and how every failed relationship or friendship in his life had been the other person's fault. He even had the gall to say at one point that none of his misdeeds were *his* fault, and he shouldn't be judged for them. Typical narcissist.

"My god, you are so *boring*. Do you even hear yourself?" Adam said. Oops again. He just couldn't help it. The guy was annoying. Minos patted his leg, and the demon behind the guy chuckled darkly, so he figured he might as well keep going.

"That 'chick with the red hair' *loved* you. And you made her doubt herself, and her beauty, and lied to her about the future, all for what? Some sex? To make you feel good about yourself? You dated her for almost a year and broke up with her in the meanest way possible because she, what, questioned you? Asked if you guys were gonna really take that trip to Greece you kept promising her? You are such an asshole."

The guy looked totally pissed at that, and Adam just knew he was about to lash out, because that's what assholes like him did, but the demon grabbed his mouth so he couldn't talk. Adam turned to Minos, and he was feeling a little harsh, because in a few small ways this guy reminded him of Tim (only like twenty times worse, because Tim hadn't been this much of a shit, he could admit that).

"You should totally make this guy ugly. Like make his outside match his inside. And you should make him fall in love over and over and over again, and have the people he loves *never* love him back. Let them be mean and harsh and cruel like he was. And maybe eventually let each relationship last a little longer, so he has hope that things are changing, but then let each one end with him knowing they *never* loved him. Heartbreak after heartbreak after heartbreak. Let him see what it is to love someone other than himself and to find out he meant *nothing* to them."

Minos nodded his head. "It seems fitting," he said, looking at the demon, who looked gleeful. The human still looked pissed enough to come up and take a swing at Adam, but Adam wasn't worried. A few decades of actually caring about someone and having your heart broken would teach this guy a lesson.

The demon dragged the guy out, and no one else popped in. "You seem restless," Minos said.

"Well, I was thinking about sex. With you. Obviously. And it's so cool what you do and I loved sitting in and helping in any way I could, but then sex brain took over, and that guy was just kinda boring, and I was thinking about all the things we could do…" Adam trailed off as he noticed a woman gliding in. And yes, this chick *totally* glided. She was gorgeous with curly, dark hair that looked straight out of a shampoo commercial. Damn, they knew their beauty products in the afterlife.

"Minos, darling, who is your little pet?" she purred, sliding into a chair at the other end of the room, her bare leg sliding out of a slit in her dress. Damn, she could totally be a model.

"You could totally be a model. Or a statue. Like some Greco-Roman thing or something. All posed like a goddess or some shit," he said, patting Minos' thigh at the same time, because he seemed to get a little tense when the lady sat down.

"But don't worry, Big Guy, I totally prefer your dick to Greco-Roman statue girl over there. And I have *plans* for that dick. I just want her shampoo, because then you could run your hands through my hair and it would be all soft and shiny. Oh, or when you grab me by the hair, it would be like holding silk. So hot." And Adam started fanning himself a little just thinking about it.

Whatever he said eased something in the room, because Minos seemed to untense a bit, and statue lady looked suddenly less statuesque. She even pulled out some little figurine, a paintbrush, and a little palette thing with a lid. She rested the palette on the arm of the chair, uncapped it, and started painting the figurine. Where the hell had she been storing that? It wasn't big, but he had *not* seen any bulges in her dress.

49

"Is that, like, some kind of Mary Poppins dress or something? Because there were no bulges in your dress, and I am like a total pro at noticing bulges." Adam snickered. "Pun totally intended," he added.

"And holy shit, is that Minos?" Adam hopped off Minos' lap at that, to which Minos gave a bit of a growl, but he kept walking over to get a closer look.

"Oh my demon—I'm trying to not use the g-word, but I don't know if 'Oh my demon' works, ya know?" he said to the woman's bemused face. "Anyway, that thing *totally* looks like him! Fantastic! And look at the cute fangs! Minos! She's got your fangs carved in here!" he gushed, turning around to see Minos looking decidedly not thrilled.

"Oh, don't worry, Mr. Sexy Demon, you still look all menacing and evil," he said to Minos before turning back to the woman. "I'm Adam, by the way. I take it you aren't here to be judged? You aren't doing the whole kneeling and crying thing, and no demon came in with you. Are you an upstairs reject like me?"

She laughed at that, and Minos growled again, so Adam walked back over and climbed into his lap, and Minos wrapped his arms firmly around Adam, probably so he wouldn't get up again. Adam certainly didn't object. He was a *total* cuddleslut.

"I love your cuddles," he whispered to Minos, because good habits should totally be encouraged. The woman laughed loudly at that, and Minos growled again. He did not seem pleased with the woman for some reason.

"Uh oh, is she, like, some arch nemesis or something? Because you don't seem thrilled. And I can totally hate her on principle if she's on your shit list. Just let me know. I mean, I may forget and talk to her, because, hello, I'll talk to anyone, but I can *totally* do snarky when I do talk to her. I have snark. I can bring the resting bitch face." And then Adam glared at her, because it seemed fitting.

Which made her laugh again and made Minos hug him closer, but his big guy also seemed to ease up on being so tense.

"Oh darling, he is a precious pet. Wherever did you find him?" she asked.

"Oh *darling*," he said sarcastically (see, he could be snarky), "he didn't find me. I found him. And I hit on his sexy ass the minute I was dropped in for judgment. And I *am* sitting right here, so maybe stop referring to me like I'm not here or even a person. Which, I mean, maybe I'm not technically a person, since I'm dead. But you get the point.

"*And* even if you're dead, or a demon, or whatever, you ought to introduce yourself when someone introduces themself to you. And oh my god, are you from upstairs? Because you are totally giving me upstairs vibes here."

Minos laughed at that, and Ms. Darling, whose name he still didn't know, looked utterly shocked. She paused with her paintbrush an inch away from her figurine like she was literally frozen, just staring at Minos.

"This, my dear Adam, is Pandora," Minos said, waving his hand toward the woman, who still looked shocked. "And she is not an arch nemesis. She does occasionally get on my nerves, but she is harmless. No snark necessary."

"Oh, thank goodness. Because snark is hard all the time, you know? It just isn't my default state. Life's too short to be mean. Which was totally a true saying in my case, since I *am* dead."

And then a lightbulb went off in Adam's head, because he gasped, looking over at Pandora. "Oh my god! Are you THE Pandora? With the box?"

At which point Pandora sighed, sliding the figurine and paint back wherever it had come from. And didn't the paint get her dress all... painty? Because Adam thought about stuff like that. But she didn't seem worried, and he was a little preoccupied with this possibly being a mythical woman, so he figured he'd ask Minos later.

"I will never live that down," she muttered. "And listen, it wasn't like Earth was all perfect and sin-free before that anyway. And how was I supposed to know what was in the box?"

"Listen, I totally feel you," Adam cut in. "If my hubby had some secret box he didn't tell me about, you can bet your ass I'd be opening it up to see what was inside. If he had simply *told* you what was in the damn thing, it wouldn't have been a problem." Adam turned to Minos at that.

"So Mr. Sexy Demon, no secrets. Look what happens. Relationships end. Evil is released upon the world. Always bad things. No. Secrets," Adam reiterated, poking Minos in the chest on the last two words.

Minos simply chuckled. "No secrets. I may forget to tell you things, but I will never keep anything from you on purpose." And Adam figured that would have to do, so he patted Minos' chest instead of poking.

Minos turned toward Pandora. "Yes, this is THE Pandora," he said. "And no, she isn't from upstairs, although she certainly could be promoted if she wanted to be. However, she's become like a queen in Limbo, and I doubt she'll be moving along anytime soon."

"And upstairs doesn't throw parties like Limbo does," Pandora added, smiling. "I will certainly not be getting promoted, as you call it, anytime soon. I'm quite content where I am."

"Parties? Did you say parties? There are Limbo parties?" Adam asked, practically squirming in excitement. He saw Pandora grinning like she'd just won a prize, and he heard Minos groan and felt his head drop down on top of Adam's.

Ok, so he knew parties probably weren't Minos' scene, but he totally wanted to see Limbo. And Adam might be dead, but he didn't have to act like it. Fun was totally called for.

Besides, Minos had never partied with Adam. He'd show his demon a good time.

# CHAPTER 10

# MINOS

Minos despised parties.

Limbo itself wasn't so bad. There were quieter, more reflective areas, and he had visited those quite a few times over the millennia. Pandora was also correct that no one had music like they did. All the best musicians were in Limbo, and few chose to move on. He enjoyed that aspect of things.

It was just the crowds. He hated the throngs of people closing in on him. He realized as he stared at the writhing masses that it wasn't only people—quite a few demons were mixed in. Pandora hadn't lied about the upstairs crew either. Oh, they tried to hide their colorless natures with outfits and masks, but Minos could still pick them out. Pandora really had made her party section of Limbo the place to be.

Adam and Pandora were getting along like they were middle school best friends. Yes, Minos knew quite a bit about middle school. You'd be amazed how many souls he judged had started their cruelty at that age.

It occurred to Minos that it might be worthwhile to make a section of the labyrinth into a middle school. He thought reliving those years for eternity would be quite a fitting punishment for a lot of people. His musings, however, were disrupted when a demon and human almost bumped into Adam and Pandora. He growled low in their direction and they veered off with somewhat panicked looks on their faces. Good. No one needed to be bumping against his Adam. Except him, of course.

Adam and Pandora carried on, oblivious to the near collision. Despite their rocky start, which Minos knew had been mainly his fault, the two of them were now arm in arm, giggling and whispering in each other's ears, laughing loudly from time to time. Minos simply trailed behind, content to be near Adam, even if the crowds did annoy him.

He did like Pandora; he would almost count her as a friend, now that he thought about it. However, when she had entered the room, he had experienced a flare of anger that he hadn't even recognized for jealousy at first. She was a beautiful and charismatic woman, and he was a grumpy demon, and he had wondered if Adam would be better suited with someone like her. Then, when she had called Adam his pet, he had grown even angrier. He was afraid to even speak lest he say something he'd regret. However, Adam seemed to have the situation well in hand, as he so often did.

It wasn't until Adam started his 'snark,' as he called it, and decided to be mad at Pandora just in case Minos was, that Minos had fully let go of his jealousy. Adam showed zero sexual interest in Pandora, and Minos realized he was being petty. It was not something he was proud of, and he realized it was utterly absurd. He wasn't some century old demon to be acting like this. Besides, it would be good for Adam to make friends.

Minos knew his own shortcomings. He was grumpy, quiet, and reflective. He did not giggle or gossip or bounce about. Adam seemed to like him as he was; Minos knew Adam wasn't lying about that, because he literally *couldn't* lie when he was close to Minos.

Nevertheless, someone as vibrant as Adam would need a lot of interaction to thrive. Minos simply wasn't equipped with that much energy and enthusiasm. He planned on keeping Adam. Forever. In order to do that, he would need to put Adam's needs first. He enjoyed having Adam at judgment with him, and he relished the time they had spent alone, but Minos knew enough about human nature to realize that only interacting with him would not be healthy for Adam.

So here they were, at a party in Limbo. Minos wouldn't be cheery—he had no desire to try and change his very nature, and obviously Adam liked him as he was. However, he could be grumpy amongst all the people here, and he really didn't want to be separated from Adam. He could also make sure no one bothered his little human.

Case in point—Minos watched as a human began gyrating his body in their direction. Was that supposed to be dancing? The human looked utterly ridiculous. He also looked constipated. Was that supposed to be a sexy face? Being made at his Adam? Minos growled and flashed some fang at the human, who squeaked a little and possibly wet himself a bit. Oops.

Minos looked at Adam and Pandora, but they hadn't noticed. They were still gossiping and laughing, and Minos put a hand on Adam and steered him toward some seats out of the way. Pandora naturally trailed along, the two continuing to chatter away with one another. Adam obviously needed a keeper, and Minos was more than happy to accept the job.

As they sat in the comfy chairs, Minos noticed a tall, dark-haired, sexy, gorgeous human heading toward them. It only took him half a second to realize that the human was *not* a human; if he were, he wouldn't be heading towards them. Most of the demons and humans were steering clear of their corner of occupied space, although Minos could tell that everyone wanted to speak to Pandora; she was quite popular. Minos' presence stopped anyone from approaching, however, which was fine with him.

Even if the bravery of approaching hadn't given it away, he would have recognized that nature anywhere. It was held in tight control right now, but Minos still knew exactly who was heading for them. And perhaps the lust wasn't *totally* in control, because Adam smoothly slid onto Minos' lap, leaning into him languidly, even though he continued to talk to Pandora.

"Asmodeus," Minos greeted, just barely nodding his head toward the demon.

Pandora stopped talking immediately, looking at the being who had joined them. She did not look pleased, but she also wasn't naive enough to show outright displeasure.

"Asmodeus," she echoed. "How kind of you to join our revels. Is there something I can do for you?"

Before Minos could speak again, Adam jumped in. Minos was sorely tempted to slip his hand over Adam's mouth, because Az was not a demon to be trifled with. Before Minos could complete that thought, he dismissed it. He would not stifle his little human's nature. If Az caused trouble, then Minos would deal with it.

"O-M-G. You are fucking *hot*," Adam said, looking the demon up and down. Before Minos could even formulate his growl in response, he felt Adam's hand patting his thigh.

"I mean, not as hot as Mr. Sexy Broody over here, of course. But holy hell"—he stopped, looking at Minos—"can I say that? Holy hell? I mean, oxymoron or whatever, but if the g-word doesn't matter, that's ok, right?"

Minos chuckled and nodded at Adam, who then turned back toward Az. Minos also looked at Az, who was looking at Minos with a somewhat perplexed look on his face. Minos set his "resting bitch face," as Adam would call it, back into place. He'd have to remember to keep the chuckling to a minimum around other Kings of Hell. Unless he was discussing torture, of course. That always deserved an evil chuckle.

"So holy hell," Adam continued, "you are so fucking sexy. And damn, just looking at you makes me wanna ride Minos like a cowboy." Adam fanned himself a bit at that before continuing.

"I mean, I've seen his dick," Adam whispered conspiratorially towards Az. "That will be one hell of a ride. And I haven't ridden *anyone* in way too long. My ex wasn't really into penetrative sex. He was SO BORING. No giving or receiving from that asshole. I think he found it all rather messy and distasteful. Like, hello, shouldn't sex be messy? That's half the fun."

Az smirked, and Minos pulled Adam back into him. Adam almost sounded a wee bit drunk. Asmodeus could have that effect on some people, and he wasn't surprised that his little human was one of them.

"Aren't you simply delightful," Az said to Adam. He then turned to Minos. "I didn't believe the rumors circulating. The Judge of the Damned, enamored with a former mortal soul? Not just any former mortal soul, either, but a bright light of a soul? I scoffed at the lesser demons who brought me such news."

"Adam is mine," Minos stated simply. Best to establish parameters with Az from the start.

He laughed, and heads turned, staring at him with looks of raw hunger. "Adam? What a delightfully perfect name. How very fitting."

Az turned serious again then. "Don't worry, my old friend. I have not come to poach your territory." He stopped and smirked at them both then. "Although I will admit that I would gladly join the two of you. If you prefer, I could simply watch and not participate. You know how much I enjoy watching."

"No," Minos said firmly without giving Adam a chance to answer. You could not give Az an inch, because if you did, the next thing you knew you were in a full blown orgy with twenty people, bottles of oil, and gold dust that you'd find sticking to your skin for days afterwards, even after bathing. Repeatedly. Not that Minos was speaking from experience on that. Of course not.

Adam seemed content to let Minos answer. Minos also noticed that Adam's hand was slowly inching its way up Minos' thigh and toward his cock. Adam was splayed across him in such a way that he didn't think anyone would be able to see, but Az would know just the same. Minos was torn—he couldn't deny he would thoroughly enjoy Adam's hand on him, but he also didn't want to give Az the satisfaction of knowing his human was rubbing his dick. What a dilemma.

"Excuse me, my darlings, but I see someone I simply *must* dance with," Pandora interrupted. Minos had almost forgotten about her presence. He looked at her; she was flushed and more than likely turned on. Her gaze was focused on someone in the crowd, and without another word, she was up and out into the throngs.

"Oh yeah girl!" Adam called after her. "You get some! Have fun! You only live once! Or, umm, die once?" Adam sort of trailed off. Yes, he was definitely slightly intoxicated by the lust in the air. His face of confusion cleared enough for him to sit up and yell out, "Sex it up, girl!" He then collapsed back into Minos and put his hand on Minos' thigh, letting it continue its journey up toward his dick.

Az smirked again, looking pointedly at where Adam's hand had disappeared, blocked from view. Upper demon could be so annoying.

"No, Az. No watching. No orgy. No oil. And *definitely* no gold dust," Minos said, throwing in a little growl for good measure.

"Ah, yes, the gold dust was an unfortunate choice, I admit. Originally I was only planning on watching, as you know. The gold dust seemed like a good idea. A way to spot all the participants afterwards. Who knew we would both become so... involved." Az merely shrugged.

At that moment, Adam's hand did indeed find Minos' cock, which had hardened in order to meet his hand halfway. Minos was accommodating like that, after all. Adam only barely rubbed up against him over his pants, but he still had to stop himself from groaning or splaying his legs wider so Adam had better access.

"It looks like our party time in Limbo is closing. I have to say, it wasn't really lovely to see you, Az. Although you did cut our party time short, so perhaps that was worth you coming over to say hello. If you came for gossip, then, yes, I have acquired a formerly mortal soul. He is mine. There will be no sharing. There will be no stealing. Is that all? Because if so, as I said, there will be no watching, and we will be leaving you here to cause whatever havoc you have come to cause."

Adam's hand was slowly, maddeningly rubbing across Minos' dick. Adam looked blissed out, and every few passes over his dick, Adam's hand would gently close around Minos and squeeze, making Minos' eyes want to roll back in his head in pleasure.

Asmodeus slid forward, closer to Minos, who was about to growl out a warning, but then he began to speak quietly to Minos, his eyes firmly looking at Minos' face. "I came to see, yes. I also came to offer, because I would never turn down a threesome, an orgy, or watching such lovely creatures as the two of you have a sexy time."

Az put his hand up to forestall Minos' reply. "I hesitantly accept that you do not wish that, but in a few centuries, when you want to spice things up, remember that my mere presence as a watcher will make things infinitely more... interesting." Az smirked at that, but then his face grew serious again.

"I also came to give you a warning," Az continued, still looking at Minos' face. "They're here," he breathed out.

With that, Az gave one final look, filled with longing and lechery, at Adam and Minos, and then he got up and departed.

*Well shit*, Minos thought. "They" could only mean one thing. Someone on the leadership team had gotten wind of what was going on, and like locusts descending in a plague, the soul-flow coordinators were on their way. The bureaucratic cockroaches of the afterlife were about to descend, and Minos and Adam needed to be far, far away before that happened.

# CHAPTER 11
# ADAM

Adam had never been so horny in his entire life. Like, not *ever*. He felt like he could literally cum in his pants just from rubbing Minos' dick over his breeches. Just feeling all that long, hard thickness, thinking about holding it in his hand, fantasizing about sucking on it, tasting the precum and rubbing Minos' balls while he did it. He could imagine that thick, hard cock working its way slowly, excruciatingly slowly, into his ass, until it hit him just right and he was full of nothing but Minos...

"Holy shit, we gotta get outta here Minos. Because I need to taste you and get fucked so bad right now. Like I don't think I've ever needed anything more." Adam gave Minos' cock a nice firm squeeze at that, and since that other demon dude had just walked away, Minos let out a lovely little groan.

Before Adam could even squeak in surprise he was picked up and cradled in Minos' arms. His dick was hard and he was guessing Minos was also putting on quite the show for anyone who happened to glance at them, but Minos didn't seem to care, so Adam didn't care either. Minos was up and walking very quickly toward the door to the judgment room, and people and demons alike were clearing the way.

"Look at you, big guy. Clear those crowds so you can fuck me senseless. Hell yeah." Adam snuggled into Minos, one arm draped over Minos' shoulder and the other splayed across his chest. And ok, maybe he also played with Minos' nipple a bit. Because it was there, and it was a hard little peak, and Minos was a huge, hulking, sexy piece of burgundy demon, so Adam couldn't help playing.

"Holy fuck, you are hot, and I am horny. Will you fuck me, Minos?"

"Yes, little one. You only need tell me what you want, and it shall be yours," Minos groaned out. And wasn't that the hottest thing he ever heard.

"I wanna be skin to skin with all that sexy manhood... err, demonhood. Whatever. I want all the skin and touching and licking. I want you to throw me down on the bed and feast on me. I want you to play with my ass and stretch me out and get me ready for your huge cock. I wanna feel you slide inside me, until there's nothing but you. Until it's all I can feel or think about. I want you to use me like I'm your toy. I wanna give you pleasure, and have you touch me and play with me and get off in me.

"Holy shit, I want that. I can practically feel you in me just thinking about it, your dick sliding in and out, your arms wrapped around me, squeezing my nipples and pumping my cock, until we both cum everywhere.

"I have never been so horny Minos. What the fuck. It's like I'm gonna spontaneously explode in orgasm just thinking about it."

Minos groaned again. "I'm sorry, little one. Az is a lust demon. He has that effect on mortals. He takes away inhibitions. The further away you get, the less the impact will be. I don't want you doing anything you don't want to do, so we can wait until your mind is clear."

Adam groaned then. "Ok, consent is super hot, but rest assured I *definitely* want everything I just said. I wanted that before Mr. Lusty sat down to chat with us. I just didn't feel this... urgency. So fuck away, sexy guy. Ravish me like I'm a 19th century virginal governess in a Harlequin romance novel. I am *so* ready for it."

Minos' look of slight confusion probably meant he wasn't familiar with Adam's reference, but Adam had been pretty damn explicit before that, so he figured he'd get exactly what he needed. It was a shame, though, that demons didn't get to sneak their mother's soft core porn books in order to learn all about sex when they were probably way too young to be reading that shit.

Adam wasn't sure how they were already walking through the hellscape and up to Minos' house—he knew they had been moving fast, but he didn't think they were moving *that* fast. But he also hadn't felt himself fade out and in. Maybe Minos had some other demon-power way to get around? Whatever the case, it was *not* Adam's primary concern at the moment.

Nakedness.

That was Adam's primary concern. Skin pressing against skin. *Now.*

They were barely through the door before Adam was out of Minos' arms. It was kind of a flailing jump-fall out of his arms, but Adam didn't care. He had priorities, and being graceful was not one of them. He had his shirt off and was yanking off his pants as he walked toward the bedroom. He heard Minos behind him along with the sound of clothes, so he figured his demon was on the same page.

He hadn't been fucked in... years. Jesus, it had actually been years. It *almost* made Adam pause. He'd played with toys, of course, but Tim hadn't been into anal. And Minos was *big*. But Adam trusted that Minos would make it good for him. Minos had done nothing but make *everything* so far good for Adam. And Adam knew that Minos wouldn't hurt him. Well, maybe only in a good way, if Adam asked for it. Adam almost chuckled to himself at that.

But then they were in the bedroom, and it was like everything was happening too fast, or in stop motion, because Adam was so fucking horny he could barely think straight. As soon as they walked in Adam turned around and sank down in front of Minos, taking Minos' hard-on into his mouth, moaning at all that hard, thick skin and the taste of his sweet precum on Adam's tongue. And Minos was moaning, his hand sweeping through Adam's hair, gently cupping his head.

"Demons, Adam, you are amazing. So beautiful. So good for me."

Adam moaned again, long and low, ready to cum just from hearing those words. Adam didn't even realize he had such a praise kink until Minos had started talking to him when they'd done the mutual blowjob thing. Holy shit, Minos praising him just totally did it for him. He thought one tug and he'd cum, and he was about to reach down and touch himself, but Minos pulled him up and tossed him on the bed.

Like, actually tossed him. And it was fucking hot, because the bed was soft, and Minos' eyes were literally glowing, his hard cock thrusting out in front of him, and Adam felt like he was the main course in a gourmet meal. He groaned and felt a little precum dribble out of his dick, and Minos looked at it and licked his lips. And holy shit, Adam was on *fire*.

And then Minos had Adam's cock in his mouth, and the warm, wet, heat was too good.

"Shit, shit, holy shit, Minos, you're gonna make me cum."

Minos pulled off just long enough to say, "Yes, be my good little human and cum in my mouth. Don't worry—I know you'll be able to give me more than one orgasm tonight."

And yup, that totally did it for Adam, because when Minos' mouth wrapped around his dick and Minos hand wrapped around his balls, Adam was cumming. He groaned, his upper body pulling off the bed with the force of his orgasm. It felt like he was pumping his soul out through his cock, the orgasm was so strong, and he yelled out. The pleasure went on, longer than he was used to, Minos still gently suckling on him.

And then he fell back down on the bed, feeling drained, and yet he was still somehow half hard in Minos' mouth. As Minos gently sucked on him and he floated in a haze of bliss, he felt his arousal coming back.

As if sensing the start of that restless energy again, Minos growled, "Roll over for me, my perfect little human." And then he helped shift Adam onto his stomach, raising his hips slightly off the bed, pulling his body back to the edge like it belonged to him.

And Adam and his body did belong to Minos. Totally and completely.

"Are you sure, little one?" Minos asked, gently rubbing his ass, down his thighs, then up underneath to gently squeeze his cock, and finally back to his ass. And Adam's arousal spiked hot and strong again, uncontrollable, and he writhed under Minos' hands.

"Yes, please. Please, please, please. I need... I need something. Please, Minos. I need." He didn't even know what he needed, except more.

And then Minos' hand came down lightly, slapping Adam's ass, a quick, sharp sting, and Adam gasped at the sensation, moaning, and pushed his ass back for more.

"Do you like that, little one? So perfect for me."

And all Adam could do was moan and push back again, wanting more of anything Minos could give him. He felt another sharp sting, and then there was warmth and pleasure as Minos' hands rubbed around his ass. Adam was quivering in anticipation.

"Please. Please, Minos. Fuck me. Please fuck me."

And then Minos' tongue was licking his asshole, gliding across his hole, spearing into him, loosening him up. Adam had forgotten how good this felt, the pleasure of being licked there. His dick was so hard it practically hurt, and Minos' hands were grasping his butt, pulling his cheeks apart, and he was sucking on Adam's hole, and all Adam could do was moan and undulate underneath the onslaught. Holy shit, it felt so good. And then something was reaching around, underneath him, circling around his dick, and Adam was so blissed out that he couldn't even process what was happening for a moment, because Minos' tongue and hands were all accounted for.

"Oh my god, your tail. Holy fuck, Minos, your tail," Adam groaned out. And Minos chuckled as he licked, and Adam felt the reverberations through his skin. His tail, warm and soft yet also firm, slowly wrapped around Adam's dick, all the way from top to bottom, and began to squeeze in a gentle upward movement, and the tip thinned and brushed against the top of his cock. Adam almost screamed out in pleasure as he felt it probe gently at his slit. He had never felt anything like it.

Adam realized he was panting and saying "Please, please, please," over and over again. "Please fuck me, Minos," he cried out. Because it was too much but also not enough, and he needed to be filled up. He needed Minos inside of him. He wanted to feel owned by his demon.

"You want this, my human? You want my cock inside your ass? You want me to stretch you out?" Minos asked, his fingers now gently rubbing against Adam's ass, one slipping inside, slicked up. Adam had no idea where the lube (or whatever the hell it was) came from, and in that moment he didn't give a shit. Because Minos' finger was *big*, and it was slipping inside him, stretching him out, and he groaned, feeling a sting and a pressure, and it was still not enough. He canted his hips back, and Minos' tail firmed on Adam's dick, pulling him forward again by his dick, and *holy shit*.

"Yes, yes, I want this. I need you inside me. Need to feel you. Need to be owned by you."

And then two fingers were in him, and he was *so full*, and all he could do was groan again. He felt like his world began and ended where Minos' fingers were stretching out his ass and where Minos' tail was wrapped around his cock. He was nothing but sensation and feeling, just a floaty haze with no words, no thoughts beyond the pressure and pleasure.

And then the fingers were gone, but before he could voice a complaint, Minos was entering him. And if he had thought two fingers felt full, *holy fuck*, Minos was big. He panted, feeling the stretch, the burn, but Minos' hands were pressing against his back, smoothing down his ass and pressing lightly down, centering him as Minos stayed still, letting him get used to the feeling.

"Breathe, little one, and know I will stop at any moment. Relax and breathe. Such a good human. You just tell me if it's too much. Be my good little one and breathe for me," Minos groaned out.

And holy hell, consent was sexy as fuck. Because Adam knew Minos would stop in a heartbeat, and the burning eased as he felt his body relax under Minos' hands and words. The pressure was still there, but the sting faded, and he moved his hips back again, thrilled to once again feel Minos' tail clamp down on his cock. All he could do was moan as he felt Minos slide deeper. He had never been so full.

"Look at you, Adam, taking my cock. You got it all, baby. Look at you. So good for me."

Adam moaned again, because he literally couldn't form words if he wanted to. He was so full, his ass and his cock and his balls all tingling in pleasure, and Minos was sliding his dick in and out, hitting spots inside Adam that sent bolts of pleasure ricocheting through his body.

Adam was panting, pushing his ass back into Minos to meet his thrusts, but also so he could feel the exquisite pull of Minos' tail on his dick as he did it, like he was jerking himself off with the tail at the same time he was meeting Minos' cock in his ass. And then Minos reached down and took Adam's hair in his hands, gently pulling his head up, wrapping his other arm around Adam's chest and bringing him onto his knees and up against Minos' body, wrapping him tightly in his embrace.

"So beautiful. So perfect. Mine. Forever mine," Minos growled out in Adam's ear. And that was all it took. Adam felt his orgasm explode out of him, cum shooting out of his cock as Minos' tail squeezed and his dick pressed deeply into Adam.

Minos' arms held tighter, crushing Adam against him, and he felt the cock in his ass pulse deep inside. Knowing that he made Minos cum sent another spurt of cum out of his own dick.

Minos was kissing his ear, whispering in it, "Yes, so beautiful. Mine. So good for me, baby."

His tail had loosened around most of Adam's dick, but he realized it was still firmly gripped at the bottom of his shaft, and somehow, Adam was still hard. He felt a little sore, but the crazy sensitivity he got after cumming wasn't there. Minos was slowly drawing himself out of Adam's ass, and he gave a little mewl of disappointment.

Minos chuckled, "Oh, we aren't done yet. I know you have one more in you for me."

"Oh my god, Minos, I don't think I can cum again. You'll kill me," Adam moaned out. But he wasn't so sure, because his dick *was* hard, and his ass felt empty, and he was sore, yet it was that good kind of sore, and he really did want more. He wanted to feel Minos for days.

Minos chuckled again, and it was the best sound Adam had ever heard. "Still not quite god, my sweet little one, but I'll be your god if you'd like to call me that. As for another orgasm—you've been around a lust demon. Besides, you're already dead."

Adam huffed out a surprised laugh. He had kind of forgotten about being dead, because he had, weirdly enough, never felt so alive.

Then Minos' tail unwrapped and Adam squeaked as Minos turned him around and literally threw him backwards to the top of the bed. And it was *still* totally fucking hot that Minos was that strong and could manhandle him like that.

Plus, holy hell, the view. Adam was splayed on his back, resting up on his elbows so he could take it in. He felt like a virginal sacrifice looking up at Minos. All that burgundy skin and muscle was towering over Adam. Minos' dick was still hard, jutting out, glistening with cum and lube or whatever the hell he had used to enter Adam. His tail was undulating next to him gently, and Adam couldn't help staring at it, thinking about what it had done to him.

And then that tail was slithering across the bed, up toward Adam, and his legs splayed open without conscious thought as he watched it. It was impossibly long, and it kept coming, yet Minos wasn't moving.

"Look at me, little one." And Adam did, staring into Minos' eyes. "Do you know what my tail was used for?" Minos asked.

Adam didn't, but he continued to stare, his gaze locked on Minos', as he felt the tail brush up against his hole, gently caressing. He gave a little mewl again as he felt it enter him, slowly pushing in, and it was like it was waving gently inside him. He felt his dick grow harder and a bead of precum leak out the top. He couldn't believe he had any cum left in him, but impossibly, he did.

Holy shit. That tail. It was touching him inside, moving, prodding, gently easing forward, finding every place that felt good and exerting pressure. He could feel when it hit his prostate, and Adam moaned as it began pressing there.

"For a few centuries, I used my tail to indicate which level of hell someone belonged on. It grew to wrap around the human, and each time it encircled them, it indicated a lower level. My tail could grow to be very long, encircling a man up to nine times. Tell me, Adam, how naughty have you been?" Minos asked playfully, yet the look in his eyes was scorching.

Adam groaned again as the tail pressed deeper into his ass, yet it still continued to press against his prostate at the same time. He couldn't take his eyes off Minos. If he looked down he knew he'd cum, and he didn't want the exquisite pleasure to end. And still it went deeper, until it was almost too much, and Adam moaned out, his upper body falling back against the bed, his eyes shutting in ecstasy that bordered on pain.

"So deep. Minos, you're so deep. I can't. Oh my god, Minos," Adam panted out. But when the tail began to withdraw, Adam groaned in protest. Minos wasn't done though—his tail slowly began fucking Adam, never going deeper than the point that was Adam's limit.

He could feel the bed dip and knew Minos was crawling up toward him. His eyes were closed, yet he could still picture Minos stalking him like some kind of feral beast, eyes glowing as they watched Adam writhing on the bed under the onslaught. Then a hand was on his dick, holding it firmly at the bottom of his shaft, preventing him from cumming, and another hand was fondling his balls.

Adam felt Minos press in, close to his body, and he opened his eyes to see a wicked grin and a hint of fang, and then Minos' head was coming down toward Adam's chest, and he felt a soft bite at his nipple. His body arched up without thought and he yelled out.

"Oh god, Minos, Oh god. Holy shit. I can't. I'm gonna cum. Oh god, I'm gonna cum." Adam was panting and groaning and humping his body against Minos' tail, and that mouth came down and bit his other nipple, and the pleasure was so sharp it was almost pain, or maybe the pain was so soft that it was pleasure, Adam didn't even know. All he knew was that he was all sensations, his body alive to every touch. He felt like he was on the verge of an orgasm, but Minos held him there, the hand around the base of his cock preventing it. The feelings were so intense, so good, that he felt his eyes tear up.

"Minos!" he cried out as he felt that mouth bite down on his neck, teeth stinging and mouth sucking. "Please, Minos, please!"

He couldn't. It was too much, too good. Then he felt the tail pull from his body and Minos' hands move from his dick and balls, but before he could even groan in protest, Minos' cock was entering him in one swift move, and his tail was wrapped around Adam's dick again, and he felt Minos' mouth on his. Adam opened his mouth on a groan and Minos' tongue slipped inside, and Adam sucked on it frantically. Then Minos' teeth were nipping his lip, gently nibbling and biting and pulling before letting go. Everywhere on his body was like one giant nerve ending.

"Open your eyes for me, little one," Minos growled out.

Adam did. Minos was above him, pumping in and out of Adam's ass, and his tail was squeezing Adam's cock, and it was *so much*. It took effort for him to keep his eyes open, but he did, and his gaze locked with Minos.

Adam realized again that Minos' eyes were never black. There were galaxies in those eyes. Stars and infinity floating in the darkness. He gazed into them and was overwhelmed with the pleasure of his body, but he felt like something was happening to his soul, too. He was lost inside Minos, and he could tell Minos was lost inside his gaze as well.

Minos languidly pumped in and out Adam's ass, that tail squeezing, one arm supporting his weight as he touched Adam everywhere with his other hand—rubbing down his arm, over his chest, cupping Adam's face in his hand. And Adam was caressing Minos everywhere he could reach as they stared into one another's eyes.

It was bliss, and it felt like it lasted eons. Adam almost wanted to cry from the sheer beauty of it. He never wanted it to end.

Eventually, though, Adam felt his arousal building impossibly higher. Then Minos was speeding up, pumping harder into Adam's ass, the tail squeezing in time to his thrusts.

"Yes, little one, look at me. Look at me and tell me. Tell me, Adam. Be good for me and tell me."

"Minos, you feel so good," Adam moaned out. He was so close, so close to cumming again. And his heart felt like it was going to burst out of his chest; everything he ever was and ever would be belonged to this demon.

"Your body is perfection. You're sucking my cock in, humping against me. Look at you, so lost in your pleasure. You're so beautiful, little one," Minos groaned. The words made Adam ever hotter, and his hands gripped both Minos' arms where they had caged around Adam to support Minos as he pumped harder and looked down into Adam's eyes, their mouths close enough to pass their breaths back and forth.

"Tell me, baby. Tell me," Minos ground out, and Adam could see the pleasure overtaking him as well.

"I love you," Adam cried out, staring into Minos' eyes, and he wanted to shut his own eyes because the feeling was so overwhelming, so much. If he wasn't dead he thought it would've killed him.

"Tell me again," Minos gritted out.

"I love you. I love you. Oh god, Minos, I love you," he chanted, and then he was cumming again, his gaze locked on Minos', and he felt Minos pump into him one final time, and the pressure in him increased and he knew Minos was cumming inside him again.

"Minos!" he cried out, somehow still cumming, like his orgasm would never end.

"Yes, little one. Mine. You are mine now. Forever."

And then Adam's orgasm was finally fading, and his eyes closed against his will in exhaustion, and he felt Minos' tail loosen, his cock being pulled from Adam's ass, and he groaned a little, but then he was wrapped in Minos' arms, his face pressed against Minos' chest, totally enveloped by him.

He was warm, and finally sated. His body was like a separate entity from him; he had no energy to even move. But wrapped in Minos' arms, he had no desire to go anywhere. Behind his closed eyes he could still see Minos' gaze—those eyes filled with galaxies, staring at Adam, staring into his very soul.

Adam sighed and drifted off to sleep, knowing he was safer and more cared for than he had ever been in his entire existence.

# CHAPTER 12
# MINOS

Minos was dozing, which was a strange thing for him. He occasionally slept, but mostly he chose not to. Having Adam curled up in his arms, however, softly breathing against his chest, had lulled him into a light slumber.

Yet something had woken him, and it took him a minute to realize it was the soft chiming that was coming from the other room. Adam stirred against him, and he cursed the leadership team in his head. Nothing should disturb his precious human.

His human who had told Minos he loved him.

Minos had lived for millenia; he was beyond time. Sometimes he forgot where or when it had all even started. To live so long was to let memories fade into the ether and embrace each experience as if it were new. It was finding twisted pleasure in coming up with a particularly fitting punishment, or even experiencing blinding frustration in dealing with the upstairs crew and all their damn rules.

Yet most of his experiences were not new. Variations, perhaps, on things that had happened before, but he thought he had experienced all that was to be had in pleasure and pain during his endless existence. After all, how could he come up with fitting judgments if he himself had not experienced despair, hopelessness, and anguish? He preferred to let those memories fade away, but the feelings they had evoked were always with him, making him better at his job.

Minos had thought there were no surprises left for him. He had been wrong.

In all his memories, in all his time, he had never had someone be in love with him. Yes, he had loved and been loved. He had friends. Demons he was close to. Perhaps they never said the words to one another, but there was love there of the familial type.

But what Adam felt for him? What he saw in Adam's eyes as he had told Minos he loved him? Minos had never seen that. He had never felt that type of love and devotion from anyone. It was like someone was ripping a hole in his chest and yet filling him up until he was bursting at the same time. It was breath-taking and overwhelming and amazing but also painful and frightening in a way that Minos had never felt. Demons, it hurt.

Because if anything happened to Adam, he would end the world.

The chiming raised slightly in volume, and Adam stirred against him again, moaning softly and then using his tongue to lick across Minos' nipple. Minos smiled, running his hand through his human's hair.

"Did you sleep well, little one?" he asked. "You were so beautiful for me." He felt Adam grinning against his skin at that. His human loved to be praised, and Minos would give him all the praise he could possibly want.

"Holy shit, Minos. That was... like, wow. Holy shit. And your tail. And your dick. And your tongue. And just like... holy shit. I'm speech-less. We are *definitely* going to do that again," Adam said, his voice muffled by Minos' chest before he shot up to look at him. Minos chuckled as Adam wiggled a little and then continued to talk, because his little human was never really speechless.

"And I am so sore, but like totally in a good way. It feels awesome. Like I was well used. Because holy shit, I *was* well used. Excellent job, big guy. Ten out of ten stars. No, like, a million out of ten stars. And we need snacks now. Because sex then snacks, you know? Even though we don't *need* snacks, they would be awesome. And we can cuddle in bed and eat some unhealthy shit, although that doesn't really matter because I'm dead and you're like this super hot demon, and..." Adam trailed off, cocking his head.

"Minos, I think your living room is chiming," he said, and then he was off the bed and out into the other room.

Minos sighed. He had hoped to put things off a little longer, but Az had warned him. He slowly got himself out of bed, not looking forward to the message that was awaiting him.

"Um, Minos? You have, like, writing on your window? And it's chiming? And it's also on your ceiling, I think? And it looks like it's appearing across the counter in here too? Holy shit, it's like aggressive email. Will it just keep showing up everywhere until you read it?" Adam asked.

"Unfortunately, yes. The chiming will also get louder until you can't hear anything above it. That takes a day or so though," Minos replied. "The writing will also appear on every surface no matter where you are by that point."

Adam snorted at that as Minos walked into the living room. "Because of course you would leave shit unread that long even though it's annoying as fuck. Why not just get it over with?"

"Because, my dearest human, sometimes you just don't want to hear from the Leadership Team. They are pompous, overblown bureaucrats, and they bring nothing but aggravation. Luce and Yah both utterly regret their creation."

"Yah?" Adam asked. Minos merely pointed a finger up, and Adam replied, "Ohhhh. Yah. Got it."

"Go ahead and read it to me if you'd like. That will satisfy the message, and I'm sure you're curious about what's in it."

"I am *so* fucking curious, but I didn't want to overstep or anything. But I am nosy as fuck," Adam giggled out.

Minos walked over and took Adam into his arms, looking into his eyes. "You can never overstep. There is nothing I would keep from you, nothing you cannot know. I will always try to spare you from hearing the worst of humanity in the judgment room, because you have a soft and shining heart, but every part of my existence is open to you."

Adam smiled, reached up, and pulled Minos' lips down to his. What started as a soft kiss was soon full blown making out, until the chiming ratcheted up another notch, at which Adam pulled back.

"Ok. Just, like, read it out loud?" he asked.

"Yes. I shall procure us some 'snacks' while you do so," Minos replied.

Adam snorted again. "Procure us some snacks, then big guy. I love you. And you're so sexy with your fancy talk," Adam said, smiling over at Minos before looking back at the message on the window.

Minos was momentarily halted by how casually Adam just said he loved him. He knew it to be true; Adam hadn't lied during sex, because Minos could sense those things. Still, he had not expected to receive the gift of those words again so soon. Adam was a continuous gift, however, so perhaps he should not have been surprised.

Minos walked over and thought about what constituted snacks, listening as Adam began to read.

"*Attention All Non-Mortal Souls: This is a reminder that soul-flow coordinators are an integral part of the afterlife experience to all levels. Moving souls to their appropriate afterlife locations is the goal of all afterlife workers, and soul-flow coordinators ensure that no mortal souls are left waiting in the queue for too long. They serve an important role in keeping things running smoothly.*

"*If you are assigned a soul from a soul-flow coordinator, please remember that this soul is a priority and should be treated as such. If the soul has been misplaced, please try to assist them. If that is not possible, please send them to the appropriate department to be processed.*

"*Soul-flow coordinators are **not** to be ignored, and no soul that is assigned from the queue should **ever** be returned to the queue unprocessed. Please remember that soul-flow coordinators have the full support and backing of the Leadership Team. Any directive that comes from them should* *be handled as if it is coming directly from above and treated with the utmost seriousness."*

Minos couldn't help it, he snorted and rolled his eyes. Adam stopped reading to look at him. "Man, that's some pompous shit, Minos. No wonder you don't want to read their messages. I once worked for a telemarketing company, and I think management may have almost been as assholey as these guys."

Minos chuckled. "Yes, telemarketing came from them, so that isn't surprising."

Adam whistled, then continued reading the letter. "*It has also come to the Leadership Team's attention that the following souls have been misplaced. If they are in your department, please direct them immediately to the appropriate department for assistance.*"

"Then there's like a bunch of numbers and stuff, do you need me to read those?" Adam asked, looking at Minos. Minos shook his head no and read over the list of numbers himself. Sure enough, Adam's soul was in the list. Shit.

Adam continued reading. "*Customer satisfaction is our goal. Together, we can make the afterlife experience exactly what it needs to be for each soul. Cooperation, especially with soul-flow coordinators, is essential for this process.*

"*Thank you for your serious attention to these matters. Sincerely, The Leadership Team.*"

"Holy shit, Minos, the 'Leadership Team' is full of assholes," Adam said, doing his adorable air quote thing. Minos heartily agreed.

"They are indeed. Unfortunately, however, we do have a slight problem." The message was fading from the glass as Minos walked over to the window. "Your soul was on the missing soul list," he stated.

"Oh *hell no*," Adam snapped. Minos loved his little human's fiery nature. "I am *not* going back upstairs. The Leadership Team can go fuck themselves."

"No, you are not going back upstairs. Your place is with me. We will get it sorted, hopefully before the soul-flow cockroaches descend upon us," Minos declared.

He then used his finger to begin drawing runes on the glass. He hated to bother Luce in this way, but if the Leadership Team had sent out an email and identified Adam, then he knew it was only a matter of time until they tracked him here. His demons were loyal, but he had been seen by quite a few immortals from multiple departments in Limbo.

Minos wasn't particularly worried about dealing with the soul-flow coordinators. After all, if they actually had any authority or were at all effective and not ignored by almost everyone, such a message would not even have been necessary.

However, he didn't want that aggravation, and he certainly didn't want Adam upset. So he put the call into Luce, and then turned to walk over to Adam and tug him into his arms. "Brace yourself, love. We are about to take a little trip."

"Awww, you called me love," Adam gushed.

As they started to fade out of Minos' home, he heard Adam then add, "But shit, I really do hate these transitions."

# CHAPTER 13
# ADAM

A dam found himself in... an office? Like a really nice office with a killer view, but still, not what he expected for the King of Hell. He was facing a huge, shiny, gleaming black desk with a super comfy looking empty chair. There were light gray walls with bookshelves and all sorts of cool art and knick knacks he'd totally love to explore, and one whole wall was a window with an amazing view of a firefall and those awesome looking trees with the ash coating them.

"Holy shit, this view is killer!" Adam gushed.

A voice chuckled behind him. "No, that would be the view of the pits, but this one is infinitely more pleasing, I can assure you. Quieter, too."

Adam turned around to see a man in a bespoke black suit with dark hair casually standing by a gleaming black bar at the back of the office. He glided—there was no other word for it—over to the chair and gracefully sat down. And did Adam mention he looked like a man? Like, a totally super hot, runway model, underwear ad, tik tok famous hottie kinda man, but still, a man. No purple or red or magenta skin. No horns. No tail (sadly).

"Are you, like, actually Lucifer? Because I expected big hulking demon horns and fangs and maybe a tail. Because tails are just really awesome." And Adam fanned himself a little at that. "Like, *really* awesome."

The man laughed and gestured Minos and Adam toward two seats in front of his desk. Adam swore they hadn't been there a moment ago.

"I'm sorry, Luce, to call you in on this," Minos said, tugging Adam by the hand over to the seats, where Minos sat down in one and pulled Adam into his lap. Adam also swore the seat hadn't been big enough for both of them a moment ago, but it certainly was now. Hell magic was pretty cool.

Adam figured maybe he could keep his mouth shut for a few minutes so the two very important demon hotties could talk about whatever they needed to talk about. Which happened to be Adam's soul.

"I am *so* not going back upstairs. It's my soul and it is staying misplaced right here with Minos. Just so you know," he insisted, maybe a little too sternly considering he was talking to Lucifer. Also, oops. Because maybe Adam couldn't keep his mouth shut. He shrugged a little and settled into Minos' chest. At least he'd let his opinion be heard.

"Ah, I see," Lucifer replied.

Minos merely sighed, spreading his hands before going back to cradling Adam, saying, "The memo."

"Yes, I did think you were coming about the memo. The Leadership Team seems to set everyone off. They're quite insufferable. You know I'd do away with them if I could."

"Can't you throw them in the pits for a few decades?" Minos asked, and really, it was the closest thing to whining that Adam had ever heard come from his big guy's mouth.

"You know how that went last time," Lucifer huffed, his beautiful face scowling. "Morale plummeted. No one wants their torture techniques constantly critiqued. Or their levels of efficiency rated as they're trying to work. We had demons refusing to torture anyone from Leadership; they were transferring out of the pits in droves. When we had to start denying transfers, everyone started calling out for being summoned to the surface—and you know how much demons hate being summoned—but they were doing anything just to get out of work. Never mind the havoc they caused up there; we're still dealing with some of their more awful decisions.

"The Leadership demons weren't even the worst; the angels had torture demons crying in my office, Minos. *Crying in my office.* They had all the joy in their work stripped away. It took decades to get the pits right again after we removed Leadership. So no, the pits are *not* a viable option. I'm sure I don't need to remind you what happened when we put them in the labyrinth, either," Lucifer stated darkly.

Minos and Lucifer both shuddered and shared a look, and Adam couldn't imagine what was bad enough to make the King of Hell and the Judge of the Damned look so foreboding.

"Well, I mean, can't you just fire them?" Adam asked. "It doesn't sound like you like them. It doesn't sound like anyone likes them. And you're, like, the CEO, or COO, or CFO, or whatever C-letter acronym it would be for hell. So don't you get to make the rules?"

"They are, most unfortunately, a necessary evil. Yah and I tried to do it all ourselves, and in the beginning, we could. You humans simply procreate too quickly, however, and there was no way to keep up. Delegation was necessary. Unfortunately, no matter how many times we switch out the Leadership Team, they always end up this way," Lucifer sighed.

"They're awful," Minos grumbled, and yes, Adam thought his sexy demon was actually pouting. It was sort of cute.

"It's their fault there are so many souls, anyway," Minos ground out. "The hell overload is their doing—who thinks putting mosquito souls into human bodies is a good idea? Of course you're going to get bloodthirsty, annoying humans from it."

Adam stifled a chuckle as Lucifer replied, "Yes, that was one of their more unfortunate choices in soul transfers to make up for human procreation rates."

Minos continued his rant. "Maybe if they actually assisted in the workload instead of making more work, there wouldn't be 'backlog' in the queue," Minos groused, and he did Adam's thing with his fingers and air quotes. Awww, Minos was really a Mr. Grumpypants about the whole thing. But still so cute in all his pouty glory.

"You're so cute, my big, grumpy demon," Adam gushed, and then he gave Minos a quick peck on the lips before turning back to Lucifer, who looked slightly bemused by the exchange.

Lucifer clasped and folded his hands in front of him, leaning forward in his seat, staring at Minos and Adam. He was very quiet and very serious, and his eyes got kinda glowy, and Adam fidgeted a little, suddenly nervous.

"I see," Lucifer said, leaning back.

"Do you?" Minos asked, and Adam had to admit he was more than a bit lost. But he actually *did* manage to keep his mouth shut this time.

And then Lucifer turned around, made some squiggly looking gestures with his fingers on the glass, and sat back in his chair. It seemed like everyone was waiting now, and so Adam (still managing to keep his mouth shut, miracle of miracles and win for him!) curled into Minos and waited too.

There was a feeling like his ears were popping, and then he was looking at another absolutely gorgeous, model-worthy, sexy as hell... ummm... man? Woman? He wasn't sure. The person looked completely androgynous to him, with a gorgeous white robe/gown kinda thing, an angular face, the lightest and most gorgeous blue eyes Adam had ever seen, and hair so light it was practically white.

"Yah, thank you for joining us," Lucifer said, and he gestured to a lovely white seat (that Adam *swore* was not there a moment ago) that was opposite Minos and Adam and yet also not too close to Lucifer.

Yah was beautiful, but also, they looked... tired. Adam figured maybe it was pretty exhausting being god. Like, that must be a hell of a lot of work. (A heaven of a lot of work?) Especially if you had to deal with assholes like that Leadership Team.

Did Adam mention how beautiful Yah was? Also, the curiosity of knowing what was under the long, white, flowing robe that Yah was wearing was starting to itch at Adam's brain. He tried to resist. He really did. This was *god*, for goodness sake.

"Ok, so what is under that robe? Because you are smoking hot, and I'm sure it's like way inappropriate to ask, but also maybe polite? Because I'd like to use the correct gender pronouns when talking to you." Adam turned red the minute he was done talking. "And I'm *so* sorry because that is so rude. But still feel totally free to answer. If you want to. Of course," he finished off lamely.

Lucifer chuckled, and Yah smiled wanly, so at least he hadn't totally offended anyone. Minos simply squeezed him tightly and kissed the side of his head, which got a look from both people—err, immortal beings?—behind the desk. It was also kind of a mind trip that there was literally darkness and light on the opposite side of the desk. Adam had to admit it was a very cool visual image.

"Minos, perhaps you ought to let your human have a little space. I had forgotten how you work on their filters," Lucifer laughed out.

"Oh no, that's totally me. I'm like this even when I'm across the room from Minos," Adam rushed out. Because he didn't want to be separated from his demon. And also, because it was totally true.

What followed was yet another discussion of the memo, which Adam half listened to. Leadership Team sucks blah blah blah, no pits for them blah blah blah. He did notice that Lucifer and Yah kept sort of glancing at each other, and their bodies were sort of shifting to face one another in a very subtle and casual manner. And he coulda sworn that there was a time or two that a hand twitched in the other one's direction.

Color Adam intrigued. Because this was way better than a Harlequin romance if 'Yah' and 'Luce' had some sort of secret crush thing going on. Talk about star-crossed lovers. And yup, that was definitely a look of longing on Yah's face when Lucifer was turned towards them.

But Adam should totally keep his mouth shut. Yup. Totally. Not gonna say a word.

"So you two are really friendly," Adam interrupted. Yeah, Adam had figured he wouldn't last long. But at least he didn't come right out and ask if they were secretly in love with one another. He counted that as a win.

Lucifer looked at Yah and Yah looked at Lucifer, and they smiled at one another. But Adam again thought how tired Yah looked, and apparently he wasn't the only one.

"You look tired, Yah," Lucifer said. Then he turned to Adam. "And yes, of course we're friendly. We've worked together since time immemorial. We forgave each other for choosing different departments to run epochs ago."

Yah sighed. "You know how it is upstairs. Some of the angels have become a bit too... unbending. As is evidenced by Adam's case, I believe. Unfortunately, he is not the only one who was 'misplaced' because mid-level management felt they weren't getting the respect they deserved from incoming souls."

Yah turned to Adam at that. "You can rest assured that heaven is a welcoming place, and you will not deal with the same placement agent as last time. They forget sometimes that not everyone has the same idea of heaven. Poor research and laziness on their part. Not everyone ascribes to biblical heavenly references, even if they are Christian."

Adam surged forward in Minos' lap. "Yeah, that's great and all, because she was a total bitch—excuse my language—but I am *not* going back upstairs. Nope. I'm staying here. With Minos. He's mine and I'm his and that's it." Adam snuggled back into Minos.

"Besides," he added, "I've been great for the judgment thing. I add some good ideas, and the demons like me. And Minos keeps me from hearing the really awful nightmare inducing stuff. So I'm having fun. And anyway, if I get to choose my heaven or whatever, then this is it. So I'm right where I belong."

"Yes, love, this is where you belong. Do not worry," Minos answered, kissing his head again. So Adam turned and gave him another peck on the lips. His demon was so sweet and protective.

Yah stared at them both for a moment, leaned forward and got the glowy eye thing going on, then leaned back and looked over at Lucifer.

"Interesting," was all he said.

"Yes, I thought so," Lucifer agreed.

Adam looked at Minos, who looked slightly perplexed, so he figured there were no answers there.

"Well, that's settled then," Lucifer said with an air of finality.

"Um, it is?" Adam asked. Because he had expected more... something. Maybe some arguing, a meeting with the 'Leadership Team,' some groveling and begging, or even some kind of angel-demon throwdown with, like, lightning bolts and fire flashing back and forth. This seemed a bit too easy.

"Yes," Lucifer said firmly. Then he looked over at Yah, and yup, there was definite affection in his gaze.

"You know I'd always be willing to swap with you for a bit. Take some of the burden. Hell is not without its trials, but a little change of scenery might be just what you need. Besides, it would shake up the Leadership Team and put them into absolute fits." Lucifer grinned at the last statement, and Yah chuckled in return.

"Ah, you do tempt me, old friend," he replied, looking back at Lucifer. And Adam was sure those two would be making out if they felt like they could. The whole god and devil thing was probably holding them both off. This was epic level romance shit right here. He (amazingly) refrained from saying something about the two of them getting a room, but it was a close call.

"I fear that the angels would revolt if we did such a thing, and you know how that goes," Yah replied, and the two of them shared a meaningful look. With one last glance of longing, Yah popped out of existence, and Lucifer turned to look at Minos and Adam.

"Wow, you should totally hit that. Because they are a hottie and there is such chemistry there!" Adam fanned himself again. "I mean, I get the whole god and devil thing kinda being an issue, but really, love is love, right? I mean, the work hours probably suck, but when you have eternity, I'm sure you could figure out schedules that work."

Lucifer chuckled again, but Adam could swear there was almost a note of sadness to it. He bet it wasn't Lucifer who was holding back.

Minos had said Lucifer was the rule breaker, and he bet Yah wasn't. But they did say opposites attracted.

"I got faith in you, Lucifer. You'll wear them down," Adam encouraged. Because he really was a sucker for a good love story and a happy ending. Speaking of...

"And we're really good? Like, Minos and I don't have to worry about being separated? Eternity together and all that?"

"Yes. You and Minos have no concern whatsoever in that area." Adam felt Minos breathe a sigh of relief behind him at Lucifer's words. He guessed he wasn't the only one who had thought more convincing would be needed.

"You may also feel free to call me Luce. Lucifer is far too formal for Minos' soul to call me. I will, of course, send a message to the Leadership Team that the misplaced soul has been placed, but you know how overzealous they get."

Lucifer then smirked when he stated, "I am, however, confident that they will get the message should they attempt to interfere with the two of you."

And on that sinister statement, Lucifer gave a positively devilish chuckle (yeah, yeah, of course the devil was devilish), turned, and squiggled his fingers on the glass. And with a little wave from Lucifer, Adam felt himself fading out of hell's corporate offices.

# CHAPTER 14
# MINOS

The next few days passed in a haze of peace and the beginnings of a routine. Minos was still hesitantly waiting for the Leadership Team to show up, and he was dreading a memo or call from the soul-flow coordinators, but so far, they hadn't heard from either.

Adam went to work with Minos, and the lower level demons had developed, amongst themselves and without any guidance from Minos, a new system of judgment. He was really quite impressed with them, and it made him appreciate them all the more. He made a mental note to do something to show how much he valued them. He knew he hadn't been the easiest to work with over the last decade or so, but they were loyal and hard-working, and they deserved recognition. He'd have to ask Adam for some ideas. His little human did seem to have some wonderfully unique thoughts on things.

Minos judged all day with Adam on his lap, and the demons made sure the first part of each working shift was populated with no souls who had engaged in extreme torture or sickening depravity that would be overly disturbing for his Adam.

The demons delighted in Adam's interjections, as well. He came up with some truly inventive, fun, and creative punishments, and they always seemed to fit the crimes perfectly. When he asked questions or made comments, he found his demons smiling and chuckling along with Adam's little outbursts. His demons were already loyal to his human, and it was all Adam's doing. He was infectious in his delight and enthusiasm.

Toward the latter half of the judging, when Adam was growing bored and distracted, Minos offered a nap or a little exploration in hell or Limbo. Adam always chose to stay with Minos, and he napped. Minos was a little surprised at how much his human slept, but Adam had simply laughed at him, saying he was used to getting seven hours of sleep and he had loved sleeping as a human, so there was no reason he couldn't love it in the afterlife too. Then he'd usually kiss Minos and make some gooey comment (which Minos secretly loved, even though he scowled) about having the perfect napping spot on Minos' lap.

At that point, Adam blissfully dozed off, and the judging of the hardcore, truly depraved souls began. Before, most demons had vied to deal with these worst offenders, for the punishments were the most extreme and often inventive. However, Minos noticed now that when they came in they looked a little sullen, and he guessed that his human's interjections and creative punishments were missed. Nevertheless, he would not subject his Adam to hearing the very worst things that humanity had to offer. His demons, apparently, agreed, for the depraved were never brought in until Adam was asleep.

When Adam awoke there was more normal human awfulness to judge, and somehow, again, his demons seemed to sense Adam's limits, for when his human was just starting to get bored, the demons stopped dropping in.

In the past, Minos had judged for days, months, even years straight. Yes, he might also have taken some prolonged vacations from judgment— everyone needed a break—but he found they were slipping into a sort of work day routine, which made sense, since it was what Adam had been used to as a human.

After judgment, they went back to Minos's home. Adam was

usually halfway naked before they'd even crossed the threshold, and Minos never complained. Adam delighted in sucking Minos off, and in sixty-nining, and he absolutely adored being rimmed and fucked. Minos was discovering that his little human thoroughly enjoyed being told what to do in the bedroom, and Minos discovered that as much as he enjoyed having his Adam service him, he also adored laying him out and completely focusing on him, feasting on him until he was a writhing, begging mess of need.

Minos cherished those moments, but even more precious were the times after. He showed Adam around hell, and his joy was contagious and made Minos see everything as if for the first time. Minos conjured a picnic by the firefall, where they talked about history and mythology, Adam utterly fascinated and hanging on Minos' every word. He showed Adam the hot springs (yes, hell had water, and yes, of course they were hot springs), and Adam debated the veracity of reality television—mostly with himself, since Minos had never watched any. It was fun for Adam to relate some of the more ridiculous events and for Minos to be able to come up with similar events from judgment. They ate food in Minos' house and cuddled on his couch. Minos conjured a television and books for Adam, who was overjoyed at both.

Minos didn't know what to make of it all. He had existed longer than his memory cared to recall, and yet it was like he was only alive for the first time now. Minos had dreamed once or twice upon a time, and his life now had that same airy, unreal quality to it that he faintly remembered from the dreamscape.

Minos kept waiting for something to happen, so after perhaps a week or two, he was unsurprised to have his snuggle time (as Adam had termed it) interrupted while they watched some television show on a network with a fruit logo—Minos had chuckled at that logo, thinking about Adam's name and now the fruit. So many strange coincidences. If he hadn't lived so long and seen so much, he would say it was more than merely coincidence, but he was old enough, and perhaps jaded enough, to know that free will always allowed for choices, and that fate was often an excuse for people to do terrible things.

"Oh demons," Adam stated. He had been trying that phrasing out lately; he said now that he'd actually met god, he figured he shouldn't be calling out their name all the time. Minos had merely chuckled and told Adam whatever he screamed out when he was cumming was fine with Minos.

Minos sighed. "Yes, I expected we would hear from them eventually. As Luce said, they are quite overzealous."

"Seriously, they can't wait? I mean, there is major drama between my favorite couple, and how could he think she'd go away for six weeks when she's starting a business? And they better not be breaking up. And can't you, like, conjure up the new season from the director or something? Because I don't think I can wait to find out what's going to happen!" Adam whined out.

Minos chuckled again. He adored how invested his little human got in these fake dramas the humans created. He had to admit, it was light, fluffy fun, and he adored hearing Adam laugh. He also had to admit to chuckling a time or two himself. Perhaps one of the saving graces of humankind was their ability to poke fun at themselves and laugh at their own natures.

"You know it will only get more insistent," Minos replied.

"Ughhhhhhh," Adam groaned out, flopping back dramatically as Minos got up to read the memo. "You read it to me. I can't. They are *so annoying.*"

Minos chuckled and cleared his throat, trying to suppress the irritation that was growing in him at just the opening line.

"*For the Attention of Minos, Judge of the Damned, an Infernal King of the Underworld:*

*The following ticket has been assigned to your department: #1618033988749894. This ticket has been misplaced and was returned to the queue as such. The soul has not been assisted, and despite the ticket number being given to numerous workers in your department, the ticket has not yet been closed out.*"

Minos paused as Adam interjected, "Is that my ticket number? That's totally my ticket number, isn't it. Bless those lovely demons of yours, Minos. They didn't turn me in for being in the wrong 'department.' They totally need a party or something. Ohhh, a party. So fun! We could do, like, demon team building!"

Adam chortled merrily, his mind off and running. "Can you imagine the demon version of a trust exercise? Oh man, that would be *so much fun* to plan. I bet they'd get hella competitive too with some team-building games. Some kind of team sporting event? Football? Eh, maybe that would get too messy. I just know someone would get gored with a horn. Oh, I got it! Dodgeball! Demon dodgeball! With water balloons or something. Filled with whipped cream! Because OMG— which does *not* count as saying their name, by the way—seeing a bunch of demons walking around looking all surly that they lost and covered in whipped cream would be freaking hilarious!" Adam ended with a giggle.

Minos chuckled again. "I'm sure they would love whatever you planned. Or rather, they'll pretend to hate it and complain endlessly, but then they'll gossip about it and poke fun at one another afterwards for decades. You may plan whatever you like, love."

"Oh, such fun! But first, focus, Adam," he murmured to himself. Then he looked at Minos. "All right, Mr. Sexy, what else do the idiots have to say about my ticket?"

Minos continued reading: "*It is imperative that all misplaced souls be properly placed. We need not remind you that customer service and keeping backlog from developing in the queue are of the utmost priorities.*

"*Please direct any questions regarding this task to the Leadership Team. We are confident that with your assistance, we will be able to drive this matter to a speedy resolution.*

"*We appreciate your sincere attention to this problem,*

"*The Soul-Flow Coordinators*"

"Oh my GAWD," Adam groaned out. Then he shot up, "Like G-A-W-D, not like the person upstairs kinda god. Anyway, seriously? Did they seriously say 'drive this matter to a speedy resolution'?" Adam did his still adorable air quotes at that line, making Minos chuckle again.

"They did indeed, my little human," Minos acknowledged, feeling his irritation fade just a bit.

"They are freaking insufferable. Newsflash—if you have to keep reminding people how important you are, then you aren't that important. What do they *do* all day? Tell other demons what to do? Instead of actually doing anything themselves? Like seriously, that is the first truly hellish thing I've experienced here in hell."

Minos scowled. "They aren't hell's creation. They're a byproduct of the Leadership Team, which encompasses all departments. I don't think hell alone could've come up with the bureaucratic shitstorm that the Leadership Team has made the Afterlife. It's a joint effort, apparently. All the worst traits of heaven, hell, and everything in between."

Minos rolled his eyes, continuing his rant. "Everyone has different values and different goals, and all they can seem to agree on is efficiency, so that's all they focus on. Luce was right, however; we needed a team to coordinate between departments. No matter how many times they get replaced, they always end up like this."

Adam sighed. "I guess man really was created in the image of all of you guys or whatever. No matter where you are, dead or alive, I guess you can count on red tape and assholery."

"Do not concern yourself with it, Adam. Luce wasn't worried, so we won't be either." At that, Minos touched the glass, did some scrolling, and found Adam's ticket in the queue. He marked it 'closed' and added no further comments. Minos knew the likelihood of that being the end of the matter were minimal, but one could hope the closed ticket would get lost in the bureaucratic shuffle and they'd be left alone.

With that, he walked over to his human, who was still draped across his couch, and in one swift pull had his pants off. Adam leaned up on his elbows and looked down his body at Minos, who was crouching above Adam's hardening dick.

"Oh, you gonna make me forget all the assholery with sex, Big Guy?

Because I am heartily behind that plan. Two thousand percent approval."

Minos chuckled, giving Adam's dick one long stroke, feeling him come to complete hardness at just that touch. "You are so easy, my little human."

Adam wiggled his eyebrows. "Ah, but you like me that way,' he said, sighing as Minos tightened his hand and started to curl his tail around his body toward Adam. Adam moaned at the sight and flopped backwards.

"Yes, little human. I love you that way," he replied. Then he lost himself in pleasuring the soul who had come to mean more than eternity to him.

# CHAPTER 15

# ADAM

Adam was... restless. The firefall picnic and hot springs and the hike through the labyrinth had all been totally amazing, and he looked forward to going back to all those places and visiting all the other hot spots in hell. Hot spots—hee hee. He'd have to use that one with Minos. His demon always appreciated his silly humor.

Minos had even mentioned that a visit "topside" would be possible if Adam really wanted, and that sounded super fun, but he didn't think he was quite ready for that yet. Maybe in a few years. Or decades. He wasn't sure he wanted to see what people he used to know were up to. He loved his life (death?) down here, and he didn't really want to revisit the one he'd had before.

What he was ready for, though, was some people time. Sure, he got lots of demon time, and for demons, they were really totally cool and nice—definitely nicer than the one angel he'd met, that was for sure. But Adam was an extrovert with a capital E, and he was ready to get out and meet and mingle. Maybe party a little. And since his last party time had been cut short, it wasn't too hard to convince Minos to take a trip to Limbo.

Yes, he knew his big guy wasn't thrilled with the idea of all those people. But he also knew Minos would do just about anything to make him happy, which was sort of amazing and trippy and mind-boggling all at once. And he also knew he'd make sure Minos had a good time. He could do all the talking for both of them, and his introverted sexy guy could just sit there looking foreboding and hot. He figured it would work out well for both of them, and they'd get nice and worked up dancing and flirting and come home and have a fantastic fuck afterwards. Which was usually what happened, anyway.

Because gah, the sex. Adam had never had such good sex. It wasn't getting old, either, and Adam couldn't imagine that ever happening. He knew Minos would be up for just about anything that Adam enjoyed. And Adam was finding he enjoyed just about anything Minos was up for. Hee hee. Pun intended again.

So Adam was absolutely giddy with fun, and with Minos looking all sexy in his black breeches, and Adam looking pretty hot himself if the look in Minos' eyes could be trusted, they made their way through the judgment room and into Limbo.

He didn't know if Pandora had some notification system or what, but not two minutes after they'd stepped through the door of the nightclub atmosphere and found exceptional seats (Minos might have growled a bit), she appeared at their table and sat down with them.

"Holy shit," Adam gushed, looking at the stage that they had a prime view of. "Is that....?" he trailed off, mouth open. "And playing with him, is that...?" He was at a loss for words. "Like seriously, holy shit! Talk about a mix of musical decades! They sound freaking amazing though!"

Pandora laughed merrily. "We get all the best musicians, darling. They're too bad for upstairs, but most are not depraved enough for downstairs. Few choose reincarnation, afraid they'll lose their gifts. So they live on, as it were, here in Limbo, doing what they love.

"I suppose for them it is a sort of heaven, and perhaps that's why the soul-flow coordinators leave them alone. That, and I heard that when they last put a famous musician upstairs he caused complete upheaval. Perhaps Limbo is the heaven for wild children. It would certainly fit in my case," she smirked.

Adam laughed. "You are definitely the original wild child, Pandora."

She laughed merrily and then grabbed Adam's hand. "I sense a fellow wild child in you, darling. Come and dance with me. You can wind your sexy Judge of the Damned up so he gives you exactly what you need later." She winked at him, dragging him up and toward a throng of dancers. Minos scowled a little, but he didn't object, so Adam was off and into the masses.

Pandora was right—Adam did have some wild child him, and the atmosphere and mood were nothing short of utterly amazing. Gyrating bodies and laughing and noise and lights, and yet somehow no one ventured too close or tried to cop a feel. He could see some couples, and in some cases groups, were doing quite a bit of feeling up—and he thought maybe there was actual sex taking place quite surreptitiously over to the side. Some people watched and danced, and some people steered clear totally. But no one hassled anyone.

It was like the most amazing dancing experience ever with all the positives and none of the creepy ick factor you always seemed to end up with.

"How do you do it?" Adam yelled over the music.

"What, darling?" Pandora mouthed back, and then she dragged him off away from the stage and dancing. They were headed away from Minos, but he saw his grumpy guy talking to a demon and keeping an eye on him, so he just gave a friendly wave. Minos scowled, but Adam recognized it as his ok-fine-don't-go-far scowl, not his get-back-here scowl. (Yes, he was becoming an expert at reading scowls and chuckles and even eye rolls.)

They ended up next to a dark, polished, very fancy, very old-fashioned bar. Although he could see the dancers and the stage and Minos' horns, the sound of the dancing and the stage was completely muted. It was like he had entered a whole different establishment.

"Woah," he said, as a pale, human-looking bartender came over, placing two drinks in front of them. "This is *so* trippy. The dancers are *right there* but it's like they're in a whole different building or something."

Pandora laughed. "The magic of Limbo. I'm surprised Minos isn't over here already—he much prefers this atmosphere to the clubby one, but Zaphrael was talking his ear off, and he is a top level punishment demon, so Minos might be a minute with him. His demons so rarely see him outside of work, and they love it when they do."

She looked assessingly at Adam then. "You've been good for him. More than good for him. Transformative. All his demons do nothing but praise you." She paused then, looking into the distance.

"Minos hasn't been... himself. We all noticed it in the last decade or so. A disconnection. It was like he was fading away from us. Nothing seemed to work. But you"—she looked at Adam then—"seem to have rejuvenated him. You've brought him back to himself. No, you've made him better."

She smiled then, laughing. "But enough melodrama and feelings. Yes, the club is amazing. We keep things tame there. There is a more wild area for those who are looking for something truly outrageous, but I certainly wouldn't send you there without Minos. He's liable to kill someone if he isn't there to guard your virtue." She smirked at that.

"People in Limbo find what they need. That was what you needed tonight. And now, apparently, we need some delicious drinks," she said, taking a sip of her cocktail.

What happened next defied Adam's understanding. Pandora was there, and then she wasn't. Poof. "What the fuck?" he gaped, and then the pale bartender was standing in front of him at the bar. He swiveled in his seat, because *no, thank you*, he knew trouble when he saw it, and he was *out* of there.

But when he turned around there was a semicircle of three other pale, sort of colorless looking human-types blocking his exit, and in front of them, standing right behind his chair...

"Oh look, it's Angel-duh," he said, smirking a little at her. Because of course it was. The bitch. She was still wearing all white with perfect looking skin, but he had to admit her hair didn't look quite as in place, and her outfit didn't look quite so perfect.

"You," she seethed.

"You know, if you keep frowning like that, you're going to give that perfect skin wrinkles," Adam drawled. He did a quick scan, but unfortunately, he couldn't see Minos' face, so he doubted Minos could see him. And Pandora was *poof* gone.

"What did you do with her anyway, you bitch?" he asked. Because he liked Pandora. A lot.

Bitch Lady (Adam decided that was her new official title) waved a hand gracefully. "She was portaled elsewhere. She'll find her way back shortly. YOU, however, are another story. Do you have *any* idea what kind of trouble you've caused me?"

"Oh, I hope it's heaps of trouble. Because you were a class A bitch when I was in your office."

"You were being DIFFICULT!" she hissed, raising her voice. "You were in HEAVEN! You were supposed to be THANKFUL!"

She leaned forward, lowering her voice, and Adam backed up in his chair. Man, she was fired up. "I was demoted," she breathed out harshly. "I was *one* step away from a promotion to being a soul-flow coordinator. You were *supposed* to be sent back. You should have been *grateful*. Instead, you disappear, and we get completely stonewalled down here by all the demons, and the soul-flow coordinators are on *my* ass.

"We are going to fix this, and we are going to fix it *right now*," she insisted, grabbing Adam's arm tightly in hers. "You are going back where you belong, and I am closing the ticket, and you will be *grateful* for my assistance!"

Her hand tightened on Adam's, and... nothing happened.

Like, nothing. She kind of looked at him, and he looked at her, and she looked at the people behind her, and they looked at her, then at him, and everyone just sort of stared at one another.

Then she tightened her arm again, and gave a very deliberate blink of her eyes, mumbling a little under her breath.

Adam thought he maybe felt... something. But nothing happened, again.

"What's the matter, Angel-ughhhhhh," he mocked, drawing out the last part of her name just to see her grimace. He cheered a little at pissing her off even more. "You all out of magic mojo or something?" He giggled at that, even though he realized even if she was out of mojo, there was probably someone who wasn't.

He had no doubt whatsoever his Minos would come for him, even if he was upstairs. But he was also a very firm believer in the statement that god helps those who help themselves. He had seen Yah, after all, and they looked pretty overworked, so he figured helping himself was probably in everyone's best interest. He had no desire to be stuck anywhere for any period of time waiting to be rescued. He liked romances, but he was *not* a damsel in distress.

So when Bitch Lady turned back toward her minions to apparently confer with them, her hand got looser on his arm, and Adam took the opportunity to shoot out of his seat and out of her grasp, heading along the bar as quickly as he could. Yes, he wasn't heading toward Minos, but at this point anything away from her was a plus in his book.

One glance back showed them hot on his trail, which is exactly when he started running through the throngs of people surrounding the bar, headed as far away from Bitch Lady as possible. The bar was probably round, right? Or a big square? Eventually he'd get back around to Minos.

At least that's what Adam hoped, even though a niggling doubt reminded him that he really didn't understand how Limbo was structured. Oops.

# CHAPTER 16
# MINOS

Zaphrael was yapping away in Minos' ear. The demon was particularly passionate about one of Adam's more creative punishments, and he was expounding upon the enthusiasm the demons had for the labyrinth as of late. Minos liked Zaphrael and enjoyed chatting with him—he liked all his demons. However, his Adam and Pandora had disappeared off to the old bar, and he was itching to get over to see them.

The old bar was much more his ambiance, as well. Quieter. Less people. Although still a little too crowded for his grumpy nature. He smirked a little at that thought.

"Exactly my point!" Zaphrael burst out, and Minos gave the demon his full attention. "Sire, you are like the Judge of olden days. It is such a glory to be working with you again. We all want you to know that. Not that it wasn't always a glory, of course," the demon quickly added, backpedaling.

Minos merely raised his eyebrows, at which point Zaphrael stuttered a bit before continuing. "We are merely saying that he has been quite the boost for all of us, and it is clear for you in particular. Diasmos was even grumbling about some type of party Adam was planning, and the complaining about it has brought the entire crew closer together. He mentioned 'demon dodgeball,' but we all assured him he must have misheard."

Minos merely chuckled at that, and Zaphrael's blue skin paled a bit.

"Oh. He wasn't joking, then?" the demon muttered.

Minos rolled his eyes. "He was not. Yet I have every confidence that my demons will participate, complain endlessly, and that it will be the talk around the labyrinth for years. We will have to make sure to have shifts so everyone is forced to participate." Minos gleefully chuckled again, and Zaphrael grimaced.

"You are wonderfully devious, sire. The demons do love to have things to complain about, and this will give them endless fodder."

"They are a miserable bunch," Minos fondly said. Then, he felt something. A... pull. Like he was shifting forward just the tiniest bit, but not by his own volition.

Zaphrael must have seen or felt something as well, because his face became stricken and panicked. "Sire?" he asked.

"Something..." he started, but then he felt it again. A stronger pull. A tug, like someone was trying to move him through a portal. He let out a breath of air and centered himself, focusing on being here and now.

"Sire, is it a summoning?" Zaphrael asked, panic in his voice. "You cannot be summoned, Sire! Adam needs you here!"

"No," he stated. He had felt summonings before, and this was not it.

He took a moment to shore up his wards nevertheless. Something was very wrong. He stood, looking over to the old bar, and that was when panic hit.

Neither Pandora nor Adam were there.

They had been there mere moments ago. He had been periodically straining his head up to look over the crowds and make sure they stayed put. He knew he needed to give Adam some autonomy, yet he couldn't bear to have him too far. Staying here while they danced and then took a break had been his attempt to give his little human some space.

That would not happen again.

They were gone. The pulling sensation was also gone, but a faint taste of panic was on his tongue, and it was flavored of Adam.

Minos rose from his seat, and he unbent his form from its normal state, continuing to rise up until he grew taller than everyone, demon, angel, or human alike. He let himself nearly double in size, anger propelling his growth. His tail grew, lashing out. He let his infernal form loose upon Limbo, caring not of the panic and destruction it could cause.

He let out a low, deep growl that reverberated and echoed back through all of Limbo. People cleared the way with some overly dramatic screaming (and possibly a few bodily fluids), the music stopped, and demons came running toward him en masse.

One did not ignore the call of a king of hell.

"FIND HIM!" he roared, his voice guttural. Demons scattered, and he watched as they went in all directions to comb through Limbo.

He ignored the screaming, intent in his mind's eye of trying to place where the taste of panic was coming from. Which direction had his Adam gone? Who dared to cause him panic? His eyes glowed and his skin heated, even as he attempted to control the rage.

As he stalked toward the old bar, any stray humans ran screaming. The demons were all running to assist his search, and any angels had made themselves scarce. Then one human stepped in front of him. He almost lashed out, but he pulled himself back in time to realize that it was Pandora. She looked disheveled and panicked.

"He was in your care!" he ground out. "What happened to him! I can taste his panic!"

"I don't know!" she screamed up at him. "I was portaled out! I got back as fast as I could, but Minos, they portaled me to another part of Limbo!" her panic at that statement began to sink in.

"Minos," she cried out, placing her hands up in a placating way. "Minos, I am old. I cannot easily be portaled. You know who this must be. No one else could have given me such a concoction without me knowing."

Minos growled out his frustration, continuing to stalk to the old bar, which was in utter disarray. There was no sign of his Adam, either.

"He will be fine, Minos," she pleaded, running to keep up with him and reaching forward as if to touch him, but she thought better of the action. "They will not harm him. The Leadership Team merely thinks they're returning him to where he belongs. He will be fine, Minos," she repeated. "He will not be harmed upstairs."

Minos growled, but she continued. "Lucifer will put in the paperwork. Or go up there himself if he needs to, I'm sure. You will have your Adam back. They may not act quickly, but it will be set to rights, Minos."

Minos knew she was right, and yet... that taste of panic. He could not be separated from his Adam. He *would* not be separated from his Adam.

He could not portal upstairs. He did not have that capability. Not all angels could portal, however, and yet they were still here. He thought about that as he sniffed and tasted the air. The panic was fainter now, but he still felt it. His Adam was not close. The thought sent a spear of pain through him, but he focused on it, channeled it.

"There are passageways," he said, stopping and turning to look down at Pandora.

"What?" she asked, confused.

"There are passageways. To upstairs. And topside. And below. Scattered throughout Limbo. Not everyone can portal. There are passageways, Pandora."

She looked stricken at his statement, but she didn't deny it.

"One such passageway to hell exists in my chamber. There are others, however. The angels would have passageways as well."

Pandora slowly began to shake her head. She understood what Minos was asking.

"You are old," he continued, and he knew how disturbed she was because she did not even make a joke about him commenting on her age. "You are old, and you would know where these things are. You are the queen of Limbo, after all. You know all her secrets. All her rooms. They whisper that you helped create some of those places."

She was frantically shaking her head now, and her eyes were bright with tears. The demons around them had stopped, staring at the two of them. Minos folded his oversized form down, taking one of Pandora's hands in his. Her hands were half the size of his now. She let her hand rest limply in his, still shaking her head.

"Pandora, I need you to take me to an upstairs passageway."

"Minos," she gasped out. "They will file the paperwork. Lucifer will step in. They will fix it. *Please*, Minos," she breathed out. "*Please* don't ask this of me."

"I am sorry, Pandora, but I must. I cannot be separated from him. I can taste his panic, his anger. I am being ripped apart by being separated from him, and I must go to him *now*."

Pandora shook her head again, but Minos stated, "As Judge of the Damned, Infernal King of the Underworld, I command your mortal soul to show me to an upstairs passageway."

Minos watched as a tear leaked down Pandora's cheek, and she tightened her hand in his. "But Minos, you cannot go upstairs without dispensation."

Minos shook his head, but she continued on. "If you go through that passageway, you will be destroyed, Minos. Please, your Adam would not want that! *Please!*"

Minos merely repeated, "I command your mortal soul. Show me immediately,"

Pandora hung her head, let go of Minos' hand, and began walking with Minos following closely behind.

# CHAPTER 17
# ADAM

Trying to circle around the bar had *not* worked; it turned out that Limbo really did defy all the laws of physics and logic. Adam had ended up in a massive, beautiful library, filled with nooks and crannies and desks, and yes, there seemed to be a famous mathematician working on a whiteboard and a very famous inventor reading in a corner chair.

But Adam could barely spare them a glance. Because Bitch Lady and her drab little minions were after him, and Adam was not getting a good feeling. Panic was setting in, because he didn't know where he was, because he didn't know where Minos was, and because if they wanted to catch him they probably could have, but they didn't seem to be gaining on him, just steadily pursuing him.

And Adam has seen a few horror movies in his day, thank you very much. He always yelled at the idiots who were herded exactly where the bad guys wanted them to go, but he was finding newfound respect for the impossible situation those people were in. Being pursued by psychotic angels was stressful, and no options seemed to be the right options.

He couldn't exactly turn around, because he'd just blunder straight into them. They obviously knew the terrain better than him, so it wasn't like he could find some shortcut or take a side route. He had no weapons, and if there were demons around he totally would have asked for help, but he saw nothing but other humans. He had tried calling out once or twice, but most of them just looked up as he ran by, saw Bitch Lady and her crew behind him, and continued with what they were doing.

Apparently Limbo wasn't overflowing with Good Samaritans.

He'd then tripped out of the library and into a forest. Like an honest to goodness, lush, green forest, but it was totally overgrown and there was only one path he could take, so he took it. And at that point turning back was definitely not an option, because he couldn't have tried to maneuver around them even if he was that fast—and he didn't think he was faster than immortal beings.

Which was ridiculous, by the way. It was at that point that he slowed down, panting for breath, and just trotted along. You know what, fuck them. If he was gonna be herded somewhere, he wasn't going to get all out of breath and sweaty doing it.

Never mind that he shouldn't even be out of breath. He was dead, for goodness sake. Shouldn't he be in the best shape of his... death? Or whatever?

He turned around, walking backwards and looking at Bitch Lady.

"Hey!" he yelled. They weren't that far behind him, and they too had slowed to a walk. They did menacing really well, though, he had to admit.

"Why am I all out of breath? I'm dead! And where the hell are you leading me, anyway? Because if I weren't dead, the suspense would be killing me!" Adam chuckled a little at his own joke, but it sounded forced even to his own ears. He was definitely feeling some panic.

"In Limbo, you naturally resume the structure of your most recent living state. With practice and meditation, it is possible to revert to earlier forms of yourself. With true devotion, changing your form and overall state of being is a manageable task, but I doubt with your attention span and level of competence that you'd be able to manage such a thing," she replied snarkily.

Ouch. Bitch Lady had claws. Adam continued walking backwards, so he wasn't prepared when he stumbled into an open clearing. He sort of flailed a little as his foot caught on some tree root, and he ended up sitting firmly on his ass as Bitch Lady walked forward and towered over him.

It was a shame she was so nasty, because staring up at her, her face haloed by the sun in the blue sky above, she really did look angelic.

But looks could be deceiving. He'd take a demon with scales and horns and shifty eyes over the snarky, porcelain-skinned angel in front of him any day. At least they knew how to have fun.

"And you're being herded here," she replied, reaching down and lifting him by the arms to his feet. She was really freaking strong. She turned him around, and he saw an open door with a stairwell inside, and without another word they were marching forward and he was walking up a gray stone passageway filled with steps.

And more steps.

And more steps.

Bitch lady was always behind him, and it felt like they walked for hours, or days, and yet it also felt like just a minute before the stone turned to white walls, and the steps turned white, and they were reaching a doorway which sort of just opened in front of them.

And then there they were, back in that blindingly white office with all white furniture and the window looking outside. And yup, there were still harp-players out there. Well, fuck.

"Take a seat, please," Bitch Lady said, gesturing to the white chair in front of her desk as she rounded behind it. If Adam wasn't mistaken, the chair looked quite a bit less comfortable this time around.

He turned around, ready to make a break for it and head back down the stairs, but the door and the minions who had been following behind her were all gone. There was nothing but pristine white wall.

Well, shit.

So he rounded the desk and sat in the chair, which was definitely less comfortable than it had been. And smaller. She pulled up her tablet-looking computer thing, looked at him, and in a saccharine voice said, "Let's try this again, shall we?"

## CHAPTER 18
# MINOS

Minos knew it wasn't a good idea. He knew it, and yet it didn't matter. He needed to get to Adam *now*.

He stalked through the rooms of Limbo, close on Pandora's heels. He was seething with rage and thoughts of revenge, his insides beating in a staccato rhythm, the word, "Adam, Adam, Adam," seeming to pulsate in his very core.

Demons raced around at his feet and legs, pleading with him, yelling at him, but he paid them no mind. One flung itself in front of Minos, but he merely stepped over it. His demons were loyal, and in some deep recess of his mind, he appreciated how much they wanted to save and protect him. He felt what he now recognized as love, thanks to Adam, for his demons.

Nevertheless, he would not be forestalled. They came to a clearing in a wood, and Minos saw the glowing white doorway ahead of him. Pandora fell to her knees in the grass, tears openly streaking her cheeks. She was muttering, and he thought he heard the words, "Please don't," over and over, but he paid them no mind.

A multitude of demons flung themselves in front of the doorway, blocking the way. Minos had no patience for such things. The taste of panic had receded from his tongue, but there was an acrid, bitter flavor there now. His Adam was not hurt, but he was not happy.

Minos would see that rectified.

"You will not stop me," he pointed out to his legions. "I will enter that doorway, even if it ends in the destruction of the afterlife. No one can keep me from my Adam. He is my mate, my mortal soul, and I will not leave him with them. If it is my destruction, then I will have been destroyed of my own choice, seeking all that has brought me joy and pleasure.

"You are my demons. You have been loyal and loved. But your sire commands you to clear the way. You must obey."

With much weeping and wailing, they moved from the doorway. Despite the direness of the situation and Minos' anger, he almost rolled his eyes at their theatrics. Adam would have found it endlessly amusing to see them carrying on in such a way, and that thought brought a smirk to his face followed quickly by a flash of pain, because Adam *wasn't* here to laugh and comment over their antics.

Upstairs would pay for that.

He stalked forward, ready to open the door, when a figure stepped in front of him. As tall as him, pitch black, with wings that sometimes looked made of feathers and sometimes of steel, the demon blocked the door, casually leaning on a battle axe larger than the lesser demons who were continuing to wail in the corner of the clearing. His eyes were lighter than his skin, but only barely, and a luscious black mane of hair covered his head, along with a full beard. Minos had the thought again that Adam would have quite a bit to say about this "sexy" demon, and his wrath surged forward once again at the fact that *ADAM WAS GONE.*

"Minos, fellow king of hell, looks like you've caused quite the stir. That's usually more my thing, isn't it?" the demon asked jovially.

"Arioch, Infernal King of the Underworld, Demon of Vengeance and Chaos," Minos greeted him. "Move out of my way," he then ground out.

Minos felt his anger calm the slightest. He felt some of the rage and urgency drain from him, and he growled in response.

"You may syphon off as much of my need for revenge and chaos as you like. It will not change my mind in the matter. I will go through that door, Ari," he stated firmly. He was calmer, however, and perhaps that was not a bad thing. His resolve was stronger than ever, but blindly charging in might not have been the wisest course of action.

"Bruh, rest assured I have no desire to put a stop to what the future will bring." Arioch stopped, looking off into the distance, his eyes swirling. "Cracking, stone, blood, and a new age," he said in a dreamy voice before snapping back and looking at Minos.

"It's gonna be some good shit," he smirked, his gaze clear again. "Although your legions are out trying to find some asshole who will stop you, so I don't expect you'll have too long. No, I've come for the shitstorm. Chaos and revenge are, after all, totally my speciality." He winked at that.

Minos *almost* rolled his eyes at Arioch—Chaos always had to combine the surreal with the gritty, and it usually amused Minos, but his anger was too great for such entertainment.

"Little problem, though, asshole," Ari added. "Have you figured out how you'll get the door open?"

Minos had not. His demons could not open it, there was not an angel to be found, and he also noticed that Pandora had disappeared from the field. Perhaps she had realized the dilemma that Arioch had brought up and had left to avoid being commanded to do it. He thought she might have been able to open the door, but it was useless to try to find her now. He had no doubt she had hidden herself, and possibly anyone else who could open the door, deep within the rooms of Limbo.

Minos frowned at Ari. "I did not," he admitted.

Ari chuckled. "Revenge is an art, bruh. You gotta plan these things, not just blunder in all half-assed."

"It is not revenge I seek. I seek Adam, and there is no time for planning when they have taken him from me."

"Yes, but revenge shall come nonetheless. You shall all fulfill the roles needed of you, and I will dine on the chaos and vengeance," Ari breathed out reverently. Minos nodded his head once. Because of course he would. They had dared to take what was his.

"Then I'm totally down to help you," he added matter-of-factly. "In the spirit of vengeance and chaos, of course." He winked, drawing his axe up above his shoulders and stalking toward the closed door.

He stopped at the doorway and turned toward Minos. "Bruh, I wish I could see their fucking faces up there when you get there. I, however, have no desire to turn into billions of quarks to be spread into the universe, so I'll be hanging right here. I'm sure I'll hear the stories, though. Angels are the most ferocious gossipers."

With a dreamy smile, probably at what he considered Minos' impending destruction, he brought the axe down heavily and method-ically against the glowing, white door, the entire valley shaking and echoing with the force of his blows.

# CHAPTER 19
# ADAM

The walls were cracking. At first, he hadn't been sure what he was seeing. It kind of looked like a dark hair was stuck on the pristine, white wall. But as he'd watched (because he was completely ignoring Bitch Lady), it had spread down and gotten wider. And then another had formed. And another soon after that. He had to resist the urge to get up and feel along the cracks to make sure they were real. The window was cracking too. Hairline fractures that slowly grew longer. They were kinda forming a pretty spiderweb-like pattern on the glass, which was infinitely more interesting than the harp players outside.

Bitch Lady had begun asking him question after question, and he had given her his snarkiest, bitchiest stare down in return, refusing to answer a single one—at least out loud. Because he couldn't help keeping a running commentary in his head. *No, I don't want to garden. Playing harps looks boring as fuck. Who would want to 'relax on a cloud' for eternity when you could have demon sex instead? No, I don't want to master a new trade, unless it's sucking Minos' dick better* (he almost chuckled at that thought, but he held it in). *No, I don't need to raise farm animals or another pet.*

Although he had been super tempted to say yes, he'd like some pets, but downstairs please. Because alpacas. So soft. And cute. He wouldn't mind some alpacas. And a dog. He had managed not to say a word, however. Which was when he had directed his gaze away from Bitch Lady to ignore her completely. Honestly, the hardest part of this whole thing was probably not bursting out to tell Bitch Lady what a horrible angel she was. Adam having to give someone the silent treatment was totally a form of torture.

His not even looking at her only seemed to piss her off even more, but she just continued her questions in her saccharine sweet voice. Even though he wasn't staring at her, he could still see her, and she occasionally looked up before she seemed to compose herself and continue asking questions. He remembered the voice from above his first time around in this room, and he wondered if this call was being recorded for quality purposes. Hee hee. He hoped so. He hoped that they saw what an ineffectual, horrible angel she was.

But he had little faith in the Leadership Team based on what Yah and Luce and Minos had said. The "team" obviously had no idea what it was like to be a mortal soul. Or to be a worker bee in the whole afterlife conglomeration they had going on.

He wondered if he could lodge a complaint? They ought to have a complaint box. Adam made a mental note. When Minos came to get him—which was totally happening, Adam had no doubt at all—he was going to suggest one. For every department. And then each department could lodge complaints against the Leadership Team. And Yah and Luce could get copied on all of those complaints. And maybe corrective actions could be put in place. That would be *fun*—corrective actions for the Leadership Team. They totally needed a really long, boring sensitivity training seminar. Because those things were total torture, and they deserved it.

Adam's drifting thoughts were interrupted by a note of... something in Bitch Lady's voice. He directed his eyes back in her direction.

She was looking a little worse for wear. Her voice was taking on a strained quality, and... were those wrinkles?

Holy shit. Bitch Lady's porcelain, perfect skin had little crow's feet by her eyes. And frown lines were marred into her skin. He could actually see her pores. He stared in fascination as she seemed to slowly but surely get less angelic looking.

Then the noise started. The cracks had been continuously growing, but it seemed like only this room was affected, because everything looked fine outside the cracked window. And no one was panicking. But the cracking had been a slow, quiet process. Now, he could *hear* the cracking, along with a rhythmic thumping sound. He thought for a moment it was his heart—it felt kind of like a heartbeat, reverberating through his body—but Bitch Lady obviously felt and heard it too.

"Angel-a," a monotonous voice intoned from above. "Please advise on the status of ticket #1618033988749894. This ticket has not been closed for placement. The Leadership Team has also taken note of some... irregularities, which seem to be originating in your office."

"I don't know what's happening!" she stammered, a definite note of panic to her voice. "There appear to be cracks in the walls? And ticket #1618033988749894 is non responsive to all afterlife placement techniques."

Her voice rose in pitch as she continued, and Adam felt a twisted pleasure in her panic. "I have not been properly trained to handle issues of this magnitude. This is outside the scope of my experience and job description. I need to escalate the ticket! I cannot resolve the situation!"

With that, she put down her tablet, pushed her chair back, and glared at Adam. "This is *all your fault.*" She waved frantically around her office, beginning to shout. "ALL YOUR FAULT!" she cried out.

Adam couldn't keep his mouth shut a moment longer. "Well, maybe if you weren't such a bitch to people, and maybe if you hadn't been so damn snarky to someone *who just died* the first time I was here, then maybe you wouldn't be in this position, hmmm?"

With that, he looked up. "And *you*, Leadership Team assholes, Minos *closed* my ticket. I watched him do it. I was placed. I was placed with the approval of both your bosses, so I don't know *why in the after-*

*life* I am sitting in fucking Angel-duh's office. Maybe you should consult with *your* management, hmmm? Because you all fucked up."

The thumping was growing louder, and Adam sat back in his chair, a look of glee on his face. Because he realized what it was. It was footsteps, and a door was slowly forming on the wall. His Minos was here for him.

"Oh, you're in for it now," he chortled gleefully. "Because Minos is going to be *so pissed.*"

With that, the door was unceremoniously thrown open, and his huge, hulking sexy demon ducked into the room. Adam jumped up and threw himself up into Minos' arms. Which was quite the throwing of himself, by the way, because his demon seemed to have about doubled in size. But Minos shrunk a bit in order to catch Adam in his arms and cradle him close.

"Oh, Big Guy, you got bigger! That's gonna be fun later!" he cried out, and then they were even closer in size and Minos and Adam were frantically kissing, lips pressed together, tongues sliding into each other's mouths.

Adam sucked hard on Minos' tongue, and then Minos bit Adam's lower lip between his teeth, and they were both groaning in delight. When they finally stopped for air, they just stayed pressed mouth to open mouth, taking in each other's panting breaths.

"I'm so glad you're here, Big Guy. I fucking missed you," Adam whispered, petting his hands along every inch of face and horn he could reach as Minos squeezed him tightly.

And then all hell, or actually, he supposed all heaven, broke loose.

# CHAPTER 20
# MINOS

With his little human finally back in his arms, Minos felt a level of calm descend upon him. Adam was still blessedly Adam-like, and he looked not at all worse for wear. The room, however, did look quite a bit unheavenly.

He wondered how the cracks had occurred. Arioch had pounded away at the door, but it had seemed utterly ineffectual at the time. The door had held strong, and Minos' frustration had grown with each glancing blow against the glowing, white obstacle standing between him and his human. He had finally stalked forward and pushed Arioch out of the way, readily to bodily slam himself against the door. He had grabbed the handle, which he hadn't even seen moments before, thrown all his weight into pulling, and been utterly shocked when it simply opened up for him.

Everyone in the clearing had been dumbfounded at that. "Well," Ari had muttered, "that's delightfully unexpected." Then the demon had chortled in glee. "Oh, the chaos shall be magnificent!"

So Minos had entered the doorway and started climbing. It was quite the journey, but he plodded along methodically, feeling himself getting closer and closer to his Adam. As the walls slowly faded from

116

gray to white, he didn't let panic take hold. He took stock for burning pressure, for flames, for something blocking his way, only none of that happened. Cracks started forming in the walls as he walked, but he ignored them. If the passageway was ruined because he used it, it was the least of his concerns.

All that mattered was Adam.

When he had reached another door at the top, he had worried that this was where he would be blocked. Yet he could sense his Adam on the other side, and he had faith that a mere doorway would not be able to separate them. He expected Adam to have to open the door from his side, but he reached out to the handle anyway. To his astonishment, it opened easily, and he ducked his hulking form through it.

He had braced himself for... something. Excruciating agony. Burning flames. Dissipation. Blinding light. Bleeding from his orifices.

Demons could *not* enter heaven. This was not merely folklore. There were occasionally those who were tired of their immortality and chose to melt into the ether. A demon attempting to enter heaven was the quickest way to become, as Arioch had said, quarks spread out into the universe.

Minos had no desire to end up as such. He had thought, had hoped, that he could fight through whatever he needed to for long enough to collect his Adam and get back into the stairway. Only instead of agony and pain, he had found himself with an armful of Adam. He had immediately shrunk down to accommodate his little human, who seemed gleeful to see him. Then they were kissing, and he wasn't even sure who had started it, but he squeezed his Adam tightly and clung to him, feeling whole again, finally.

It was at that point that he registered the screaming.

The room was cracking around him and darkening from its institutionally bright white color to a more faded gray. It was also growing in size, which he expected meant they were due for some company from the Leadership Team.

The screaming was coming from a woman who was looking decidedly unangelic. She was staring at him and Adam, screaming something about not being properly trained to handle recalcitrant tickets and how demons could not be in heaven.

Minos ignored her and her tirade, looking down at his little human.

"Are you well?" he asked simply. He could see that Adam was, but he needed to check in anyway. "Shall I kill her?" he tacked on. He wasn't sure it was possible, but he could try. He knew she wasn't the force behind Adam being taken from him, but he also knew Adam disliked her and she had not been kind to him. For that alone, he would find a way to end her existence.

"Oh my sexy demon lover, I'm fine. And no, Bitch Lady does not need killing. But maybe some corrective action, huh? Because let me tell you, she *sucks* at her job. *NO ONE* should have to deal with that level of bitchiness. Especially after they just died! She has absolutely no idea what it's like to be a mortal soul. Isn't empathy supposed to be a heavenly trait or something? Because Angel-duh over there is completely missing the empathy *and* sympathy buttons.

"But you came!" he gushed, stopping his tirade to hug Minos close again. "Of course I knew you would, but I was getting *really* bored listening to all her questions. Although, speaking of, are there alpacas in hell? Or dogs? Because I think I'd like to have some. Of both.

"But anyway, that aside, I'm totally fine. A little scared when I was being herded here, but I never had any doubt you'd come for me, Big Guy. And the whole cracking the walls thing was super cool, by the way. Good work! They're totally gonna need a remodel after your visit," Adam chortled.

With that, there was a pressure change, and six angels popped into existence into the now larger room. The Leadership Team had arrived.

They were all in white suits with glowing white wings, although their hair and eye colors varied. They looked androgynous and vaguely clone-like. Minos had seen the demon part of the Leadership Team, so none of that surprised him. After working together for millenia, apparently the team started to think and act together as well. In fact, aside from coloring, the demons and angels were scarcely separable in mannerisms, speech, and attitudes.

Two of the angels held tablets, one had a briefcase, and one had a pen and notebook of some sort with an actual colorful design on it. The last was surprising. The Leadership Team was not known for being creative. Minos quickly judged based on the fact that the angel in question still looked somewhat...unique... that they were probably a new recruit to the team. He rolled his eyes, knowing that any individuality would be corporatized out of them before the decade was out.

At the arrival of the team, the female angel who had been screaming promptly shut her mouth and stood very still. She was obviously terrified, as she should be. Minos was an Infernal King of Hell, however, and there was nothing the Leadership Team could do to him.

At least he didn't think so. He was standing in heaven, after all, so it occurred to him that he might need to readjust his assumptions.

## CHAPTER 21
# ADAM

Adam felt his ears pop (sort of, because they didn't *really* pop, because, you know, he was dead), and he saw six white angels appear in the room (the white and wings were kind of the giveaway, although he had been hoping for halos too). And the room was totally bigger, too. Afterlife physics were pretty mind-bending.

Adam immediately zoned in on the angel on the end, who was standing almost an inch back from the other five. *One of these does not look like the others,* was the thought that flitted through his head.

"OMG angel person—sorry, I don't know your pronouns—but that planner is awesome! Kudos to you for the originality from your cloned compadres there. Love the rainbow swirls on it. And the pen is an awesome shade of blue."

The angel looked taken aback and almost seemed to try and cover up the design on the notebook. Poor thing. It must suck working with that crew of boring assholes.

Adam gave them a kind smile before looking up at Minos. "I totally want one. I could keep punishment ideas in it! And ideas for the exciting team-building we're going to do with the demons!" Minos looked down and smirked at Adam, nodding. Adam gave him a nice peck on the lips before directing his attention back to the angels.

Adam figured these were probably some higher up big wigs, but he was beyond giving two shits at this point. And at least Bitch Lady had stopped shrieking at them.

"So listen," he said, trying to interject some authority into his voice. He did realize that perhaps his position cuddled up in his demon's arms didn't convey the level of pissed off he was going for, but it had been a rough afternoon, and he was staying ensconced in Minos' embrace. They could just deal with it.

"I am lodging a formal complaint with the Leadership Team on behalf of ticket #1618033988749894—that's me, obviously—and I would like immediate corrective action taken for the gross mishandling of the case that was under your jurisdiction." Adam smirked at that and enjoyed the looks of bewilderment that came over the faces of the angels in front of him. He bet he just took the wind right out of their sails.

Adam knew a thing or two about corporate bullshit. He was human before this, after all. Sometimes you had to strike first and lay blame where it was due. He hated to be *that* type of customer—he prided himself on *always* being nice to anyone in customer service, because that was truly a job from hell—but he figured they were *way* past that point with this crew.

The angel in the center cleared their throat, which seemed totally unnecessary and rather pompous, and stated, "Yes, we are sorry for how Angel-a dealt with your case. You can rest assured that corrective action will be taken."

"Oh, no, no, no," Bitch Lady started mumbling out. "This was *not* my fault. He didn't want to be here. He kept insisting this wasn't his placement. I wasn't trained for this. Then I go back to get him, and a demon shows up! Demons are not supposed to be in heaven!" she wailed, getting louder and more hysterical as she went on.

Angel In Charge looked at the angel next to him, who looked at Bitch Lady. She started backing away, holding her hands up in front of her, and Adam watched in morbid fascination as she started getting grayer and wrinklier and stiffer. It was slow enough to see the process happening, but it was also done quickly enough that she couldn't even run.

Bitch Lady was now Stone Bitch Lady. Like, full statue mode.

"Ok, that is *so cool*," Adam marveled, finally hopping out of Minos' arms to go examine the statue. "You made her a Weeping Angel! Is she gonna start stealing life energy or making other people into stone? Because that wouldn't be cool, you know, and not much punishment for her." Adam ignored their bewildered looks. Obviously they weren't Dr. Who fans. Ah well, what did you expect from corporate assholes? No taste.

"But oh, she should totally have to go exist on the mortal plane or whatever you guys call it. She should have to people watch for a few decades. Get some sympathy and understanding of the souls she's supposed to be dealing with. Send her to a hospital or something. Let her see how sad it can be, but also how much hope and love people have. Because some corporate video on sensitivity training isn't going to cut it for her."

The Leadership Team continued to stare at him, bewildered, but Unique Angel (Adam really did love their rainbow planner) gave a wave of their hand, and Bitch Lady's Statue was gone. Adam smiled at them, and he thought he saw a slight upturn of mouth in response. Maybe. *There was hope for that one yet,* Adam thought.

Angel In Charge gave an offhand glare at Unique Angel, but then they glared back at Minos, ignoring Adam entirely. Yeah, that wouldn't last very long. Adam would make sure of that.

"The Leadership Team has jointly come to the conclusion that ticket #1618033988749894's gross mishandling was a byproduct of both teams, and, as such, appropriate action for the egregious error must be taken.

"It is with some regret that we must inform you that, despite your millenia of service, your recent conduct has caused us to reconsider your position. The joint divisions of the Leadership Team are afraid we must inform you that you are being let go. As such, your corporal form will fade into the ether, and a proper replacement will be found for your position.

"We thank you for your service and are sorry to have to part on such terms," the angel finished off.

Oh, hell no.

Adam started storming over to Angel In Charge, but before he got there, the angel waved their hand toward Minos with something of a smirk. Adam stopped and looked back at Minos with dread, waiting to watch him fade into the ether, or whatever the hell was about to happen. Only Minos just looked sort of bored and rolled his eyes at Angel In Charge.

Adam looked back, and Angel In Charge did *not* look amused. They waved their hand again. Then blinked. Then waved.

"Ummm, you look kind of stupid?" Adam drawled, stifling a giggle. "Just saying. Like all blinky and wavy." He couldn't help a little imitation at that, which made the angel look even more aggravated.

"Obviously you don't get to fade Minos 'into the ether'," Adam added, using his signature hand quotes. Adam giggled again, partly because the angel did look ridiculous, and partly out of sheer relief, because Adam had really thought for a moment that he was going to lose his demon.

He sauntered over and Minos promptly picked him up and cradled him. Adam gave him a big fat kiss on the lips, then he turned back to the assholes in front of him.

He probably hadn't been paying enough attention to his surroundings, because at that point he noticed that the walls were *really* cracked. Like holy shit, was the room even gonna stay standing? The cracks were speeding up, too, spreading across the walls in hairline fractures. Some were getting wider and deeper as well. And, was that...? Ewww, yep, it sure looked like blood. Leaking from the cracks. Ok, total horror movie moment now.

Based on the way that Minos was currently squeezing him tightly, he wondered if his sexy demon was somehow responsible for the demolition of this heavenly room. He couldn't blame his big guy.

"You know, you guys have gone and fucked things up good. Minos is an Infernal King of Hell, and he is probably way older than all of you, and he is probably way above your pay grade, and when we sat with Lucifer and Yahweh, they *both* said that I got to stay with Minos, and I *know* that Yah is your boss, so I don't know what makes you think you get to do whatever the hell, or heaven, you want. But you don't."

It was like using Yah's name created an instant change in the room. The Leadership Team stepped back, looking at one another and then at Adam and Minos. By the time Adam's little tirade was over, a glaring white light was filling the room.

He threw his arms over his eyes to shield them, and when he pulled them away, the angels were all on their knees, faces averted, and Yah was standing (floating, maybe?) in front of everyone. Only this was not the tired, human-looking Yah from downstairs. This was a shining, blindingly bright, scary-ass motherfucker of a Yah.

"Hey, Yah," he said, giving a little wave and getting a nod and half smile in return.

"I totally love the look. Very old testament cool. Totally bad ass. Thank god"—Adam giggled, he couldn't help it—"you showed up."

This was gonna be good, Adam just knew it. So he settled back into his demon's arms and gleefully waited for some heavenly fireworks. This was definitely a Yah you did not fuck with, and he had no doubt all would *finally* be put to rights.

# CHAPTER 22

# MINOS

There had been a brief moment when Minos had wondered if they could, in fact, terminate him. On their own, it certainly would not have been possible. Angels could not get rid of a demon, particularly not an Infernal King of the Underworld. But all areas of the Leadership Team together? Angels, demons, ghosts, the reincarnation division—well, all together they had formidable power. Certainly not more than Yah and Luce, but more than he did on his own.

Could he be recreated? That was sort of Yah's thing—creating something from nothing—so he still hadn't been too terribly concerned. Yah had given their word, and that was not a thing to be taken lightly.

Nevertheless, there had been a moment of disquiet in Minos. He knew Adam would be grief-stricken if he disappeared, and he had no desire to have his human upset for one more moment in time. So it was with some relief that nothing at all happened, and he could only roll his eyes to show Adam that he was absolutely fine and there was no reason to worry.

He had forgotten the whole god's name thing, too. Upstairs that was a thing—you were not supposed to use god's true name. He was actually pretty sure Luce had started that at a point in history when angels and humankind were both equally demanding of Yah's time, and Yah was conscientious and caring enough to always come when called. Luce was always saying Yah was too kind for their own good, and then somehow he had made it so that you did *not* say god's true name. Luce didn't bother with his own name, because he felt no need to answer when called. Invoking Lucifer was as likely to get you engulfed in flames as it was to get you an actual visit.

If Minos had thought of it himself, he would have simply invoked Yah's name from the start as soon as he entered the door. Though Minos hated to bother them, Yah would clear this mess up.

Alas, living for all eternity meant things occasionally slipped your mind.

Yah was here now, however, and it was certainly not a pleased god looking down at their Leadership Team.

Minos smirked with grim delight, clutching Adam tightly in his arms, which was exactly where he belonged, as the voice of the Leadership Team began rushing out explanations.

"Most High and Majestic Creator, we can assure you that we did not invoke your name in this small matter that shall shortly be driven to a satisfactory resolution. It is a minor inconvenience"—Adam huffed at that statement—"of a misplaced soul and a negligent placement angel which are being handled. The soul is being accorded to their proper afterlife designation, and the placement angel has been properly disciplined for their actions. Rest assured that the write-up for their errors shall be handled and filed in due course.

"As for the...ahh..."—the angel looked up and glared at Minos at this—"*demon* that is apparently in heaven, we are most aggrieved to say we have no idea how such a thing has occurred, but you can once again rest assured that the security team will be addressed for their dereliction of duties in regards to this."

Yah simply stared down at the kneeling angels, saying nothing.

"Oh, you guys are *in for it*," Adam chortled. His little human was really very gleeful about this entire incident.

The angel glared up at Adam this time, and Minos growled low in his throat. Adam merely patted Minos' chest, however.

"Where, exactly, were you planning on placing this soul?" Yah asked in an eerily calm voice.

"Oh, that is definitely the voice your momma uses when you have made a big ass fucking mistake and are about to find out exactly how you fucked up," Adam laughed. Yah simply smiled at his Adam again. None of the angels dared look on the face of god, so Minos supposed it didn't break the "bad ass" look Adam was so impressed with.

"Almighty Majesty on High, the soul was placed in heaven. We were reallocating them to their original designation, as per their arrival ticket."

"I see," replied Yah. "Did anyone double check the soul's placement ticket?"

The angels startled at that, and there was some bustling and whispering and a briefcase opened up and tablets came out, and Minos could appreciate the comedic aspect of this all happening while the angels were kneeling.

Then there was some frantic whispering and conferring while Yah strolled over to Adam and Minos.

"I see you two look no worse for your ordeal," Yah stated. "Although the same cannot be said for this portion of heaven," they pointed out, quirking an eyebrow.

Minos merely scowled a bit, but as he watched the walls quickly set themselves to right and the room took on its heavenly, white glow once more.

"Ah, Honored and Beatific Creator?" came a trembling voice from the group of angels. It seemed that they were making the newbie give the bad news and setting them up as the sacrificial lamb. The angel with the planner Adam wanted (and which Minos would create for him, of course) had shuffled forward on their knees at the behest of the other angels, and they looked ready to be struck down by lightning at any moment.

"Ohhh, that's my favorite Leadership Team angel!" Adam gushed. He glared at the whole group of them. "So like you to make the little sibling take the fall for your fuck-up. Moms, or Dads, always know who's *really* responsible, though. I bet little sibling gets ice cream and you all get extra chores for a week. Or a millenia. Or whatever."

"It, ah, appears that the placement did indeed change?" the angel bravely continued on. "We aren't, ah, sure how this is possible? Because it appears that the soul is still placed in heaven? But the soul is also allocated to Limbo? And the soul is also placed in hell? Which does not appear to be possible, Almighty," the angel finished off lamely.

"Mmmhmmm," Yah merely murmured.

"So you all *kidnapped* me, and you didn't even double check what you were doing? What the fuck, guys? I'm sorry, Yah, but your team definitely needs some 'discipline' for their 'dereliction of duties' in this 'small matter.'" Adam said, air quotes flying as he spoke.

"Yes, I can see that they do. Since you are clearly the wronged party here, and you have become quite adept at handling corrective action, I think your suggestions have merit," Yah stated, walking back over to the angels.

Minos wasn't aware of what corrective actions Adam had in mind, but of course Yah was.

"You shall be taking over as head of the Leadership Team," Yah declared, speaking to the newest angel. Everyone startled at that, including the angel in question, who dropped their planner and their pen and *almost* looked up at Yah but averted their eyes at the last minute.

"The rest of you shall be undergoing some sensitivity training. Adam has some thoughts in mind. I'm sure he'll be able to compose a memo with all the details with the help of the Judge of the Damned. There shall also be something called "complaint boxes" at all levels.

"The Leadership Team has gone unchecked for too long. You may be a necessary evil, but you are not the ones who are in charge here. I think you have forgotten that there are things out of the realm of your authority. You have forgotten that we are here to serve, not to claim power. You shall be reminded of your place."

Yah looked over at Adam and Minos, and a door opened behind them. "I expect you'll want to find yourselves back home. I trust the trip back shall be less eventful than the trip here."

"But, Almighty..." the previous mouth-piece angel said. They just couldn't let it go, obviously. "Almighty, how...? It isn't possible...?" the angel stuttered.

"Of course it is. Adam is Minos' mortal soul. Thus, they cannot be separated, Minos cannot be terminated, and they may go wherever they would like. It is really quite simple. If you had just done your jobs correctly, you would have realized that."

With that cryptic statement, the angels all turned to gape at Adam and Minos, and Yah disappeared from the room.

## CHAPTER 23
# ADAM

*Minos can't have a mortal soul*, blah blah blah. *We would never have tried to destroy a soul*, blah blah blah. *This wasn't our fault*, blah blah blah. *No precedent for such a thing*, blah blah blah.

Adam mostly tuned out all the hubbub that erupted after Yah left. He snuggled into his demon. Huh, Minos really *was* his demon. And he was really Minos' human. Because he was, like, apparently his soul or some such thing. Or they shared a soul? Or they had each other's souls? Adam wasn't really clear on the details.

And really, what did the details matter? They couldn't be separated. Ever. They could go wherever they wanted. Sounded like heaven to him.

Speaking of... "Can we please get the hell out of his place? I'm not alive anymore, but I think all this blinding white is still gonna give me a migraine," Adam complained.

Minos chuckled, utterly ignored all the apologies and questions being yelled at them, and walked through the doorway and started going down the stairs. The door firmly shut behind them, blocking out the Leadership Team and their drama (thank demons and god and Yah and Luce and whoever else).

"Oh, we are gonna have fun giving them some sensitivity training, Minos. Maybe we can make them cold call souls to see their satisfaction with their experience. Like telemarketing and customer service all rolled into one," Adam chuckled darkly.

"But also, they really need to loosen up. Like, we need to make them dress differently from each other and make them do some bonding time in Limbo or something. Make them take the different departments out for team morale. And of course, I'm still pretty pissed, so some torturous corporate retreat is totally in order."

Adam would think on it. If anyone could get the Leadership Team to shape up at least a little bit, he was confident he was up to the task. This was the afterlife, and Adam sort of thought it should be a little better than actual life. Wasn't that the point? At least for good souls.

His musings were interrupted when he noticed they were once again in front of Minos' home.

Afterlife physics. He would never get the hang of them.

They walked in, and Adam hopped down, but as much as he was ready to throw his clothes off and get fucked by his demon, he realized that Minos had been awfully quiet. Even for him. And that was saying something.

He tugged Minos over to the couch, pushed him down, and sat on his lap, at which point Minos promptly began rubbing his butt.

"Mmmmm, that's more like it, Big Guy. But you've been totally quiet."

"No more than usual," Minos replied.

"Uh, yeah, more than usual. And I'm apparently your soul or whatever, so don't try that shit with me, Mister. What's up? Were you worried? It's ok to be worried. I was totally worried, but I knew you'd come. I knew we'd be ok. Because I don't know what the hell this whole soul thing means, but I feel you."

Adam took Minos' hand and placed it over Adam's chest, his hand on top. "I feel you inside me. And apparently I always will."

"Yes," Minos muttered. "You are apparently stuck with me. For all eternity."

Adam almost jerked back at that. Apparently his Minos had some surprises for him.

"Stuck with you?!?" he repeated, practically shouting the words. "What the fuck, Minos? I am not 'stuck with you!'"

Minos smiled at Adam's air quotes, but it looked tired.

"Explain. Now," Adam insisted. Because if Minos didn't want Adam as his soul or whatever, Adam would be crushed. But he didn't think that was what was going on here. His big guy seemed... unsure of himself. It was not a look Adam liked on him.

"You are a shining soul. Pure, bright, creative. You are light in the darkness. I am... unfriendly,"—Adam chuckled at that—"grumpy, not talkative. I am a deep, endless well of scowls and grumbles. That is what you will be stuck with for all eternity. I cannot change who I am."

Adam took Minos' face in his. "Listen. You are *my* grumpy, scowly, unfriendly, not talkative demon. And those are some of the things I love the most about you.

"I love that you're all grumbles and scowls but *I* can make you chuckle. I love that you let me do all the talking, because in case you hadn't noticed, I *love* talking. I love that you're the strong silent type. I love that you will absolutely destroy anyone who bothers me or upsets me, but you take care of me utterly and completely. I love being your light in the darkness.

"You let me be me. You let me be as crazy or talkative or sex-starved or sleepy or judgmental or cheery as I want to be. You're here for me. I know you would do anything for me. You support me. Like, literally support me by carrying me around half the time," Adam laughed.

He stopped long enough to kiss his demon. "I love you. I will always love you. I don't know how or why this soul thing works, but I think it shows we are literally made for each other. I am stuck with you for all eternity, and thank fuck for that, because it is the one thing that went perfectly right in death for me."

Adam leaned back, looking into his demon's eyes. Galaxies were there. And they were all filled with love.

"I love you Minos. You are my eternity."

"As you are mine, Adam. You are my soul. I love you."

# CHAPTER 24
# MINOS

One minute they were staring into each other's eyes, and the next Minos had his mouth pressed against Adam's, their hunger a living thing that burst out of them. He licked inside of Adam's mouth, hearing his little human groan and feeling his mouth open wider. Their tongues playfully tangled, and then Adam was sucking on Minos' tongue, and he could feel the pulling sensation in every part of his body. He grabbed Adam's bottom lip between his teeth, nipping and pulling as Adam moaned louder and writhed on his lap, their dicks pressing up against one another, the pressure exquisite.

Minos used his hands to squeeze Adam's ass, caressing and rubbing the perfect globes in his hands as Adam moaned into his mouth. He lifted Adam in his arms, carrying him and still squeezing that perfect ass, devouring his mouth, leading them toward the bedroom. He needed his hands on a naked Adam now.

He tossed his Adam onto the bed, knowing how much his little human liked when he did that. Adam stared up at him hungrily as he stripped off his pants, Minos' hard-on pointing the way. He gave it one long stroke, staring at Adam, who was staring hungrily at his cock.

"Is this what you want, my soul? Do you want my cock?" Minos asked huskily.

"Oh yeah," Adam groaned.

"Tell me. Tell me what you want," Minos commanded.

"I want to suck your cock. I love feeling you in my mouth," Adam said, staring at Minos' dick. But then he looked up, flirtatiously and a bit shyly.

"What else do you want, my soul? Tell me."

"I was a little naughty, wasn't I?" Adam asked with a little wink, crawling toward Minos on the bed as he spoke. "I mean, I did go and get myself separated from you."

As Adam finished, he grabbed Minos' dick in his hand, holding the base while he licked along the top, tonguing the slit and then around the head before he opened wide and sucked Minos into his mouth. Minos could feel Adam's tongue working him as he started moving his mouth up and down. He rasped his tongue against the underside of the head, licking and suckling, letting Minos' dick get slick with his spit.

"So good," Minos ground out. "Your mouth is so good on my dick, little one. You please me so much."

Adam swallowed Minos down into his throat and moaned, and Minos felt the vibration in his cock. "Ah, my soul, such a good little human. So beautiful."

Minos put his hand on the back of Adam's head, gently cradling him as he continued to enthusiastically bob up and down. Adam used his tongue to flick Minos' slit, caressing and pulling Minos' balls as he did it. Adam stared up at Minos, and Minos was filled with such joy and love at his treasure. The pleasure was beyond eternity.

"Was my little human naughty? Does he need a spanking for running off and worrying me?" Minos asked. If Adam wanted a little spark of heat with his pleasure, Minos was more than happy to oblige. Adam's ass begged for a little pinkening.

"Mmmmmm," Adam moaned, closing his eyes and doubling his efforts at sucking Minos off. He swallowed Minos down again, and he felt Adam's throat working on the tip of his dick. He groaned loudly, and Adam responded in kind, like their pleasure was intimately connected.

He pulled Adam off him. His eyes were glazed and hazy with lust, his mouth was red, and he was panting and moaning. "You want me to spank that ass, my little human?"

"Please," Adam moaned. Minos climbed onto the bed, moving to sit at the top and pulling Adam over to him. He laid Adam across his lap, their dicks brushing against each other and causing them both to groan in pleasure. Adam looked back at Minos with a sexy smirk before he flirtatiously breathed out, "Daddy, please."

"Mmmm, yes, I like that," Minos affirmed, rubbing his little human's perfect globes while Adam humped up and down on his lap. He gave a quick slap to Adam's ass. "Be still, little one," Minos commanded. "Be still for your demon daddy."

Adam whimpered, but his hips stopped moving. Minos rubbed his ass before laying down a few quick swats. Adam groaned with each swat, and Minos watched in delight as Adam's ass took a lovely light pink hue. He spread the swats out, listening to Adam's pleasure, judging exactly the sting and heat that pleased his little human most. He could feel Adam's dick leaking precum onto his lap, and his own cock pulsed in arousal.

He reached around with this tail, and as he kept up a steady, light pattern of swats, he rubbed his tail against Adam's tight little hole, letting some slick ease the way. Adam might not understand hell physics, as he often stated, but Minos could conjure things when he needed to, and he had never been so pleased to have that skill.

Adam groaned out, pumping harder, so Minos gave him a harder swat at the same time that he pushed his tail into Adam's hole. His tail unerringly sought out and found Adam's pleasure spot and rubbed against it. Adam began pumping harder, Minos swatted harder, and both of them moaned in all the pleasure.

Then Adam was painting Minos' lap with his cum, and Minos continued to pump his tail and kept up the spanks while his lover cried out through his orgasm. As Adam's hips slowed their movement, he gentled his tail, leaving it just resting in Adam's ass. He lightly rubbed the lovely pink ass in his hands, letting Adam come back to himself.

"Oh gods and demons and everything in between," Adam mumbled into the bedding. "Holy fuck, Minos. Just... holy fuck. So fucking good."

Minos chuckled. "You don't think we're done, do you, my little human?"

# CHAPTER 25
# ADAM

Minos was going to kill him. Well, Adam was already dead, so he guessed not. But still. Best. Orgasm. Ever.

Apparently spankings really did it for him. Who knew? He floated in a post-orgasmic haze as Minos rubbed his ass, and then he felt a little twitch *inside* his ass (that tail, holy shit, that tail!), and he felt Minos' cock jerk against his lap.

And yup, afterlife recovery time was an amazing thing, because he was getting hard again. He would have been happy to suck Minos off to orgasm. Hell, he would've been happy to do anything Minos wanted him to. Minos made it all pleasurable for Adam. Giving Minos pleasure was like giving himself pleasure.

He groaned and moved his hips, thrusting back into that tail a bit. "You're not done with me. Yes, please."

And then Minos' tail was somehow impossibly wider inside him—man, he fucking loved hell physics—and he was gasping for breath, trying to keep his hips still as Minos held them down. He was *so full*. The stretch was sharp and bright and blissful even though it edged on being almost too much. "Oh god, Minos. Oh god, oh god, oh god," he cried out.

Minos chuckled, and that tail did *something* inside him, and Adam almost shot off the bed in pleasure. He would have if Minos hadn't had such a firm grip on him. Because Minos' tail was moving inside, undulating, pressing against his inner channel, caressing every inch of flesh, almost like he was being massaged by a million little fingers *inside* him, and he had never felt anything like it in his life (or death, for that matter).

"God is not here, little one, although I believe we could give even god a lesson on excellent sex."

Adam started to laugh at that, but it quickly turned into a groan. "What the fuck are you doing to me, Minos? Holy shit, I can't... It's too good. I can't, Minos."

The feeling was so intense Adam felt like he would fly apart if Minos let him go. But he knew his demon wouldn't ever let him go. He knew Minos would stop at the first hint that Adam wasn't enjoying himself, but he also knew his lover would push him to the limits of what he could enjoy. He trusted the caretaker of his soul completely, implicitly, and he knew his demon would never do anything Adam didn't want or like.

"Do you want me to stop, little one? All you need do is say so. I will never do anything you don't want," Minos said, like he could read Adam's mind. Maybe he could? And consent really was the sexiest thing ever, because it only got Adam harder to hear Minos say that.

"Minos!" Adam cried out, overcome. "Please!"

"You look so beautiful in your pleasure, my soul. So sexy and so good giving yourself up to me."

Adam would have cum again, somehow, only it was like Minos knew, because his hand gripped Adam's cock at the base and his tail slowly withdrew, which caused a whimper from Adam.

"Please, Minos,' he mewled out. "Please fuck me. I need you inside me. Need to feel your pleasure. Need to be filled with you and feel you cum in me. Please."

Minos growled and flipped Adam over so that he was quite suddenly on his back with Minos looming above him.

Adam grabbed his legs in his hands, splaying them wide and giving his demon access to his ass. Then that long, thick, perfect cock sank into him. Minos looked down at Adam and stared into his eyes, and Adam tried to look back, but his eyes rolled back and closed in the excruciating pleasure of being filled by Minos.

And then he cried out, "Minos! Holy fuck, Minos! What...?" He was panting in pleasure, unable to even ask. Because it was like Minos had a hundred little bumps all over his dick, and they were rubbing and massaging inside of Adam.

Minos chuckled darkly. "Does my little human like that?" he asked, knowing full well from the sounds that Adam was making that he most certainly *did* like that, thank you very much.

Minos was moving then, gliding in and out, slowly fucking Adam as the pleasure built and built in his body. All sensation was centered in his ass while his dick bounced between their bodies, hard and leaking precum all over the both of them.

"Look at me," Minos demanded.

Adam opened his eyes, locking his gaze with Minos', staring into the stars that shone just for him in those dark orbs.

"Say it," Minos commanded. "Tell me, little human. My soul, my beautiful one, my shining light in the darkness. Tell me."

And Minos' dick got impossibly wider as he began thrusting faster, and Adam panted, lost in those eyes, overcome with pleasure and love and endless possibilities with his perfect demon.

"Tell me, my soul. Tell me," Minos panted out.

"I love you, Minos. I love you, I love you, I love you. You are my everything. You are my eternity."

And with those words, he felt Minos jerk inside him, felt his lover fill him, and he tried to keep his eyes open to watch those stars in Minos' eyes as the cum shot from his own dick, the orgasm crashing through him. He was drowning in those eyes, in pleasure, in love. It was like they were one and the same, an endless loop of perfection.

And then, somehow, Minos went from crushing him from above to holding him pressed against his chest, and Adam couldn't help but snuggle in closer, pressing every inch of flesh possible into his demon's skin.

"I love you, Adam," Minos said, caressing Adam's skin everywhere his hands could reach. And Adam placed a kiss against Minos' chest where his face was buried, content for at least the moment to rest quietly in the afterglow of their passion.

# EPILOGUE

Adam and Minos sat at a large, comfy booth in Limbo. Adam still hadn't quite figured out afterlife physics, because although they could see the stage and hear the music, everything was muted enough for conversation. This was definitely more tolerable for his grumpy mate, and Adam still got to head into the writhing masses to dance his heart out with Pandora when the mood struck.

When they'd first arrived, Pandora had seen the two of them and promptly burst into tears, which had totally shocked Adam. She was like the ice queen, in the best possible way, of course, and the tears were totally freaky. Minos had sort of rolled his eyes, though, even while Pandora had wailed out, "I thought you were both gone! How could you make me do that, Minos? I thought I was erasing you from existence!"

Which of course required a bit of explanation. Pandora got herself under control quickly enough and got mad instead, giving Minos quite the lecture on giving her commands that might lead to his very demise. Adam had nodded, made noises of agreement, and patted Pandora's arm, but when he'd turned to look at Minos he could see his grumpy demon was completely unphased. He thought he even saw an eye roll or two.

And honestly, he figured he would have done the same thing in Minos' place, so he couldn't be mad at him. He had counted on Minos coming, and Minos had risked it all to do so. Which Adam wisely did not say to Pandora.

She ran out of steam soon enough, and Minos had grumbled out, "I do apologize for commanding you against your will. I would not have normally done such a thing, for I count you as a friend."

Pandora had airily forgiven him for his "impatience and unwise decision making," at which point Minos had merely rolled his eyes. Adam heard the apology for what it was, however, even if Pandora took it to mean that Minos had been wrong overall. Minos regretted taking away Pandora's choice. He did not regret risking it all for Adam. He didn't regret opening the door or climbing the stairs or possibly being erased, because he had to get to his love. It was all rather romantic, and Adam practically sighed dreamily just thinking about it.

They had chatted about the upstairs chaos, and it wasn't long before an impatient Pandora was pulling him towards the dance floor. He'd thought Minos would be a little more... overbearing, especially about them being separated. Adam had watched Minos' face carefully when Pandora had grabbed his hand, and Minos had grumbled a bit, but he had given a barely perceptible nod at Adam. Adam had, of course, rewarded him with a big fat kiss, and he then made sure that Minos could always see him on the dance floor.

And maybe it was Adam's imagination, but it really felt like he could feel Minos too, like a warmth in his chest. He had happily danced away with Pandora, watching as she flirted and worked her magic with everyone who danced by. And eventually he had started to miss his Minos, and he had felt that warmth tugging at him a little, so he had touched her arm and motioned back to the table.

When he arrived, Minos was sitting and chatting with a giant black demon, complete with a super sexy full-faced beard and a literal mane of black hair. Man, afterlife hair products had to be amazing. The demon also had some crazy black wings, and Adam had a hard time figuring out if they were made of feathers or of some kind of metal.

He would not ask. He would not ask.

"Ok, so what *are* the wings made of? And holy shit, or unholy shit, maybe? Your hair is gorgeous!"

Minos gave a smirk and held his arms open for Adam, so of course Adam promptly climbed into them and gave Minos a big fat kiss. The other demon laughed jovially at Adam's question.

"Thanks, Soul of Minos," the demon said. "And they are badass wings, aren't they?" he preened.

"Ohh, I like that nickname," Adam crooned, giving Minos another kiss. "I like you already," he said, turning back to the sexy demon.

"I am Arioch, Infernal King of the Underworld, Demon of Vengeance and Chaos," the demon stated, nodding at Adam with a huge smile on his face. "And totally fucking cool and not a twat like half the crew around here," he added.

"Man, you guys love your titles. And I gotta say, I was not expecting that one. Vengeance and chaos, huh? Although you totally have the biker vibe going on with all the hair and darkness and speech."

Minos rolled his eyes. "He's half-biker, half-dreamy seer. He can be infuriating to talk to sometimes."

Adam laughed and Arioch smirked, but then his eyes got sort of... swirly? And his voice got sort of dreamy, with a longing quality to it. "Such divergent paths ahead. So many endless possibilities, all leading to upheaval. One should always listen to their elders," he ended cryptically.

Then he snapped back to biker dude voice, which Adam found totally fascinating. "But Minos was just gossiping about the havoc you two caused upstairs. I can't tell you how awesome it is that your mere existence as the Soul of Minos has their panties all in a twist," Arioch snorted. "And the plans you two have for the Leadership Team? Ahhh, that is some good shit. It's gonna be epic."

Adam preened under the compliments, leaning into Minos, who gripped him tighter. Ah, his sexy Minos. So very warm and cuddly and so very fuckable... Adam looked around, suddenly feeling suspicious, because he was feeling really damn horny all of a sudden.

"Az?" Adam called out. Arioch roared out with laughter and Minos merely rolled his eyes.

"Azzy, you asshole, the Soul of Minos ain't putting up with your shit," he said, looking out into the crowd.

And yup, there he was, Mr. Lusty Pants. Adam giggled a little at that thought as Az came over and sat beside Arioch, casually throwing an arm behind the hulking demon.

"Have I missed the orgy?" Az asked with a wicked grin.

"No orgies," Minos replied firmly.

Adam gave him a little pat on the chest. Oops, did he accidentally brush against his nipple while he did? Oops, did he wiggle a little on Minos' hardening cock?

Minos groaned but then said, "No orgies," firmly again. "Rein yourself in, Az."

Az literally pouted. "You are simply no fun. Don't I at least get to watch a little foreplay? It would be something new and exciting down here," he sighed out.

Arioch raised his eyebrow at that. "Awww, Azzy, you bored? Your kinky orgies aren't doing it for you anymore?" Then Arioch laughed in a maniacal way, which Adam had to admit was a little weird, but neither Az nor Minos seemed the least bit phased by it.

Az sighed. "Everyone here in Limbo has at least seen it all, even if they haven't done it all. It's not me who's jaded." He visibly gave himself a shake. "Trust me, I shall never grow dissatisfied with sex. I was simply looking for something... different."

As if his words had done something—and perhaps they had, Adam didn't know how afterlife physics, nevermind afterlife magic—worked, Az grabbed onto Arioch's hand with one of his and clutched his chest with the other hand.

Minos leaned forward, clutching Adam tightly, an air of urgency to his posture.

"What's going on?" Adam asked, utterly perplexed.

"It's..." Az looked up, wiggling his fingers over his chest. They looked somehow less substantial than they had a moment ago. "It's a summoning," he finished off, surprise evident in his face.

"About time! Let the pandemonium set in!" Arioch chortled, but the other two ignored him.

"You can't be summoned topside! You're an Infernal King of the Underworld" Minos grated out. (Adam almost rolled his own eyes at that statement. Demons and their titles.)

Both demons started to rise, Adam still ensconced in Minos' arms. Adam wasn't sure what they were gonna do, because yeah, Az was actually sort of fading, very slowly, and Adam didn't know how you grabbed onto someone who was literally fading.

Az merely smirked and waved them back down, letting go of Arioch's hand. His hand was insubstantial enough that he didn't know there was much choice in the matter.

"Calm, my old friends," he smirked. "Perhaps the powers that be have found something exciting for me to do topside. I was just bemoaning Limbo, after all. I sense no ill will in the summoning, although certainly there will be some questions as to how I was called upon." Az frowned a little at that, but it quickly cleared, and he chortled.

"Besides, you know that no summoning circle can hold me. This shall be fun," he said gleefully.

Arioch and Minos both sat back down, and Arioch chuckled. "Ah yes, that was a few centuries ago when a mortal tried summoning you and you decided to go, wasn't it? Didn't they die from cumming so much? Although I have a feeling this will be quite a bit different," he finished with a smirk.

Az laughed. "Not dead. Nearly, but I left them alive. Quite satisfied as well. That was an entertaining afternoon. I'm sure I'll be back in a few hours, and perhaps I'll have an interesting story to share upon my return. And I wouldn't count on things being too different," he winked. It was as if his decision to embrace the summoning made it final, and he was gone.

"Ah," Arioch sighed out, "you guys really are shit-stirrers. How fantastic! You're going to make things entertaining down here." With that, Arioch walked away from them toward the stage. Adam could only imagine what trouble he was about to start.

"That's not very fair," Adam pouted. "We didn't make Az get summoned."

Minos chuckled at Adam, gripping him tightly, and oops, had Minos just rubbed against Adam's nipple while he did it? And were Minos' hips slowly pushing his cock up into Adam's ass?

"No, we did not, my little human, but I am not sorry to have to you myself again."

Adam turned in Minos' lap and straddled him, and they both groaned as their cocks rubbed at each other through their clothes. He took both his hands and placed them on Minos' face, caressing his scruff, up his head, and along his horns. He stared into Minos' eyes. Galaxies there, and all for him.

"I love you, my soul," Minos said.

Adam pressed his lips firmly against Minos, a hard, quick kiss. "I love you. You are my eternity. Now take me home, Minos."

Minos picked him up, and Adam snuggled into his demon's chest. Adam thought about how it seemed so very long ago that he had been a human staring heartbrokenly at some silly text messages. Who knew dying would be the best thing to ever happen in his life?

He and Minos had so many fun things to do together. An eternity of possibilities. And Adam guessed with friends like Arioch and Az, and a Leadership Team to deal with, and judgments to be handed out, and endless kinky sex to be had, it would be the most perfect eternity he ever could have imagined.

Turns out his soul had found the perfect afterlife placement after all. Because that's what Minos was to him. His heaven.

Keep Reading for a preview from the next M/M paranormal romance in the Demonic Disasters and Afterlife Adventures Series from Shannon Mae

*A Beginner's Guide to Mistakenly Summoned Demons and Other Misadventures*

# SNEAK PEEK
## A BEGINNER'S GUIDE TO MISTAKENLY SUMMONED DEMONS AND OTHER MISADVENTURES

### Gabriel

Grams was brewing something in the kitchen again.

Gabe had stopped by after he finished teaching his last class; he'd needed a little dose of Grams to get him through the rest of the week. School politics and troubled students weighed on his mind, and the woman who raised him was always good for cheering him up.

When he'd walked into the kitchen, however, he'd seen the farmhouse table strewn with herbs and plants and random things he didn't want to look too closely at (he thought there might have been a small bowl of dead flies, and possibly a bag of toenail clippings), and he'd looked toward the stove to see the giant stock pot on it.

Gabe thought he might have PTSD from that stock pot.

So he'd given Grams a kiss on the cheek and hightailed it out the back door to the garden, where he was currently kneeling on a pink flowered cushion and pulling weeds (he hoped they were weeds, anyway—he was kind of hopeless at gardening).

He was not going to ask what she was doing. Nothing good ever came of Grams working in the kitchen.

"Gabey, honey, can you come help me in the kitchen?" her voice called out. Grams had a lovely voice, sweet and melodic and cheery. Gabe shuddered nonetheless. He dragged himself to his feet, turning toward the kitchen like a man about to walk to the gallows.

Those words *never* ended well for the person 'helping.' By eight years old he had already known that the stock pot was trouble—they'd already had the thing living in the basement for almost a year at that point—but he'd also enjoyed some of the babysitters Grams had cooked up into watching them.

But when he was in third grade, he had come home from school dejected and sullen, claiming that he didn't have any friends. He was being melodramatic after being left out of a playground game, whining about how he wasn't popular and his life was miserable. So Grams had started cooking, asking him to help as she did. Nothing much seemed to happen, and he was a bit disappointed in the lack of fire (they had three extinguishers), smoke, or crazy, horrible smells (they'd once had to stay in a hotel for three days).

Then he'd gone to school the next day. Everyone had been super nice to him all morning. It had been great. Until the playground. Jack B and Marty had literally gotten into a fist fight over who was his best friend, Carly and Jessica had both been sobbing because he wasn't playing with them, and Donny had held onto his clothes and refused to let go, eventually tearing his shirt and scratching him up.

Grams had picked him up early, tsked at the wreck he was, and they'd cooked again when they'd gotten home (he definitely had to be persuaded).

All she'd said after was, "Sometimes a wish is a curse."

He wasn't sure if teaching him a lesson was her goal all along or if she was actually trying to make him popular. Either way, he was cautious after that.

Then there was the frog. That was fourth grade, he thought? Everyone got to take home the class pet, and he'd been thrilled. But he had bemoaned the frog's plain, boring features, and Gram had worked in the kitchen, and he had a bright orange and blue frog (which he had thought was totally cool). But his teacher of course refused to take it back, claiming it was NOT the original frog, and he would not send some "poisonous prank" to the next person watching the pet. So they'd gone to the pet store and bought a replacement for class, and he'd kept the colorful version.

Mr. Frog (he had been nine—originality was not his forte) was still alive. Twenty years later and he figured it probably shouldn't be, but he just kept feeding it, and maybe they had the occasional movie night together (Mr. Frog loved horror movies). If it ever did die (which Gabe kinda doubted would happen at this point), he'd be pretty devastated.

But the thing living in the basement aside, and the really bad babysitter that had hosted the house party aside (RIP to all their pet fish), he still hadn't been totally ruined by Grams in the kitchen.

It was the chicken that did that.

Try having a headless chicken running around your backyard for three days.

THREE DAYS.

He still couldn't eat chicken if he thought about it too much. He'd gone vegetarian for a year after that, as had his brother and sister. His sister, Seraphina, had stuck with it, but he and Michael eventually ate meat again. Sometimes, though, he'd think about that chicken... and yeah, he had some definite food issues.

The list went on from there, but he and his siblings had all been more than a little traumatized after that.

But asking Grams not to brew something up was like asking the rain not to fall. It was going to happen eventually no matter what you did, so you might as well just try and plan for it and hope you didn't get stuck in the downpour.

"Gabey? Honey?" she called out the kitchen window. He was wool-gathering, and he reluctantly dragged his feet the rest of the way into the house, stepping just inside the back door and no further. He was staying far away from the stove and the crock pot if he could help it.

She turned toward him. She looked like she belonged on a baking show. A short (at least to him), slightly plump (in that perfect grandma kinda way), white-haired woman with laugh lines and a face full of sunshine. She even had an apron on that said, "Many Have Eaten Here, Few Have Died." He kind of snorted when he saw it, because Grams did like to be witty.

He pointed to the apron. "I think the thing in the basement might disagree."

She tsked him. "It didn't die, honey. Honestly, no matter how many times I tell you kids, you insist on thinking the worst. When it tried to eat Seraphina's friend, I realized it may not have been the best pet to keep, but it's not like I sent it to the shelter to be euthanized. Of course I found it a good home."

Gabe merely nodded. It was like she was talking about a dog who had accidentally bit a guest in the house.

"Anyway," she added darkly, "that Chloe was a bad apple. I think it might have been on to something trying to bite her. Did you see she was just arrested again for selling crystal meth? A bad apple, that one." She tsked again before really looking at Gabe. He felt like she could see the day's stress on him.

She frowned a little, walked over, and gave him a pat on the arm. "Oh honey, you look tired. Those kids of yours giving you a hard time? You know I keep telling you that you need to get out more. Relieve some stress. You can't make your job your whole life. You need to find some nice young woman—or man—to get your mind off things."

She winked at him lasciviously, which was more than a little creepy. "You know I heard there's a sex club that opened up in the city. A nice little orgy might be just what you need."

"Grams," he groaned out.

"I'm just saying. Sex is healthy. Just make sure you use protection." She paused, thinking a moment. "And you kids might want to clear my browser history without looking at it when I die. Just a heads up."

"You're never dying," he scoffed. "You're like a virus. You'll live forever, infecting people with your cheer and insane ideas."

"Oh, honey," she beamed, "you say the sweetest things. But," she continued, all business now, "I do need some help. This stock pot is simply too heavy, and it's a dud, so I need the contents disposed of, and I just can't lift it." And then she smiled at him.

Gabe did not trust that smile. Not even a little bit.

"I just need you to go pour it out in the backyard. Go out past the vegetables and away from the trees please. And make sure you pour it in a good circle to deactivate it. You remember what happened the last time it was poured out in a line."

Gabe shuddered. He had blocked out the locust incident until she brought it up. That had been Serphina's fault, because she'd been in her teenage phase of doing a half-assed job at everything, and they'd found the bugs all over for days. He squirmed a little thinking of them crawling into his clothes.

"A closed circle, Grams. I got it," he sighed out.

He went to grab the stock pot, but she put a hand up. "One more thing," she said, walking over to the table, writing something on a piece of parchment, and then walking over to drop it into the pot. She brushed her hands together. "All set!" she smiled.

He still didn't trust that smile.

She frowned at him. "I just had to deactivate it. Now go on. Don't keep it waiting. Never know what will happen if you do," she scolded.

So he grabbed the pot by the handles, which mysteriously always stayed cool to the touch. He studiously avoided looking at the contents. He did *not* want to know. It was heavy, but he kept in decent shape, and he managed to lug it out to the yard without spilling a drop. By the time he got to the back of the property, he was puffing a bit, but he stopped, rested the pot on the ground, and caught his breath.

Best not to rush these things.

He planned out the circle, picked up the pot, and started walking and pouring over the slight lip on the side of the pot, being careful not to splash it up onto himself. It was hard work with a full pot, but by halfway around the circle it was lighter and easier. He kept the same pace anyway, being sure not to say anything or even think too hard about anything other than forming a circle. The liquid was a red color, but he tried not to notice too much. Although it did smell really good.

He couldn't figure out exactly like what, either. Sometimes it was like fresh baked cookies, sometimes he got a whiff of cinnamon, or vanilla, and even fresh rain and the smell of an autumn morning was in there.

He timed it perfectly to finish the circle with the last bit of liquid. He stepped back, put the pot on the ground, and admired the rather perfect circle he had poured out.

The rather perfect circle that was still clearly visible since the liquid was not seeping into the ground.

The rather perfect circle that was now shimmering slightly inside, and where there was no longer any grass, just dirt.

The rather perfect circle that quite suddenly had a man standing inside of it. He was tall, probably over six feet, with black hair, a sculpted, somewhat androgynous face that was all sharp angles, and a lean body. He appeared to be wearing leather pants, but he was barefoot with no shirt. Gabe didn't usually see people as sexual beings—that just wasn't how he worked—but he could appreciate that this guy was aesthetically pleasing and beautiful, like a work of art.

The guy cocked his hip a little and was lazily smirking at Gabe. It was the sinful smirk that gave him away, because there were certainly no horns, or a tail, or the odd skin color.

"Grams," he yelled, "you've summoned a demon again."

Preorder Book Two HERE.

# Note from Shannon

Dear Reader,

I hope you enjoyed your time with Adam and Minos as much as I did. I found their personalities endlessly entertaining, and they even surprised me a time or two (apparently characters have a way of doing that, even to their authors). It's amazing to me how they took shape and took on lives and personalities of their own.

Along with those two came a fun cast of side characters, and some of those characters will be getting books in the near future. They're already jabbering away in my head, so expect to hear from them soon. (Poor Az doesn't know what he's in for!)

If you enjoyed this book, or even if you didn't, please leave a review! Reviews and word of mouth recommendations are the best resources self-published authors have. Knowing that I have made someone smile or laugh or escape their problems for even a minute is motivation to continue to write. So thank you for reading - I appreciate you!

Happy Reading!
Shannon Mae

# ABOUT THE AUTHOR

Shannon Mae began her journey in the M/M romance world as an avid reader, then a beta reader, and eventually an editor who works with the unparalleled Tammy B. PA from Aspen Tree E.A.S.

When a dear friend suggested she should write her own book, she decided to do just that. She gravitates to writing paranormal romance, since that genre is her first love, and her books tend to be low-angst and filled with happily-ever-afters.

She is an unfailing optimist with a side of snark and sarcasm. When she isn't editing, writing, or working her day job, which she loves, you'll find her on some outdoor adventure or embarking on a hands-on project (that is probably slightly more complex than she thought it was).

She lives in a small, seaside town on the east coast, and she spends her free time with her eye-rolling, sassy teenage daughter and her adorably loving dog.

Life is a place full of mysteries and wonders, and she hopes to capture that joy and fun in her writing. Adding some fun, sexy times makes it all complete.

Shannon Mae loves hearing from readers!

Visit Shannon's website: www.shannonmaeauthor.weebly.com
    Join Shannon Mae's Menagerie for all the fun stuff!

Made in the USA
Monee, IL
27 June 2023

37805783R10095